THE PIOUS DANCE

OTHER BOOKS BY KLAUS MANN

Mephisto

Pathetic Symphony

The Turning Point

Andre Gide and the Crisis of Modern Thought

THE PIOUS DANCE

The Adventure Story of a Young Man

Klaus Mann

Translated by Laurence Senelick

PAJ PUBLICATIONS
NEW YORK

Originally published in German under the title *Der Fromme Tanz*.
Copyright © by Ellermann Verlag, Munchen 19.

Library of Congress Cataloging in Publication Data
The Pious Dance
Library of Congress Catalog Card No.: 87-81205
ISBN: 1-55554-017-1

Printed in the United States of America

Publication of this book has been made possible in part by grants received from
the National Endowment for the Arts, Washington, D.C., a federal agency, and
the New York State Council on the Arts.

For Anna Pamela Wedekind

You cannot be, you can but waste yourself,
You cannot rest, but must wander to the ends of the earth.
You cannot get, for all gold turns to lead,
Nor nothing know, for it will be a cheat.—
You can but live. And living is enough.
        Saying of Ernst Bertram

One of us *must* sing the song, *our* song.
Who is it to be?
        Anya and Esther

FOREWORD

Beginning a book with a "Foreword" means attempting to explain the book. Anyone who feels he has to explain his work and his efforts is also confessing the need to apologize for them.

Perhaps no book needs to apologize more for its confusion at the very start than one which issues from our younger generation, deals with our younger generation and wants to be nothing more than an interpretation, expression, description and confession of that younger generation, its urgency, its perplexity—and perhaps its high hopes.

"I shall be the occasion of a great deal of reproach," states the first sentence of a deeply moving novel by a seventeen-year-old in France. "But what can I do about it? Is it my fault that I was twelve years old a few months before war was declared? No doubt the confusions that followed in the wake of this extraordinary time were such as no one had ever experienced at that age. Nor was I the only one."—So writes Raymond Radiguet, who was doomed to die at the age of twenty.

There is no reason for us to plead our cause to those who hate us and wish us ill. They could not care less, even though they are in the vast majority. Nor could we care less about staving off their "great deal of reproach" or even confuting the reproaches we "are the occasions of" ourselves. But we ask those who freely empathize and sympathize to be indulgent to our effort, which is conscious of its lack of polish; the clarity it gropes for never appears or develops fully. I am sure that most of the book's artistic defects derive precisely from that cause: too often there is a discussion, an accusation or a debate, where only an image or a form should exist. And, like Radiguet in France, the explanation I offer for it all is the grand historical one. How can I help it if my hero Andreas and his contemporaries were thirteen years old when the revolution, that other event fraught with consequences, began?

Every so often it strikes me that if a young man today is still writing books, that in itself is a basic sign of retardation and depression. The younger generation no longer puts much stock in an interest in books. I believe there are only isolated cases still extant of an enthusiasm for the importance and necessity of books. Other things take pride of place.

I am not sure that one can put these "other," book-hating things into a book after all or can describe them in a refined manner. With this uncertainty I have undertaken that hazardous enterprise. Perhaps the ardor and the problem of this dubious and optimistic "Postwar Generation" will not be shaped and formed but only perpetuated in this work. Perhaps this generation has not produced an idiosyncratically characteristic work so far simply because, all appearances to the contrary, it doesn't need one.

My "adventure story" is filled with such questions, such ideas, often expressed much too directly and circumstantially.

For I cannot offer this book as either the "expression" or the "formulation" of the younger generation. Perhaps it can stand as a document, so that "the confusions that followed in the wake of this extraordinary time" will find only too clear a reflection in it.

But may I also hope that the thing I have no word for and therefore call the new innocence, the new faith, the new piety sends a faint glimmer of light through these confusions?

I shall be grateful to anyone who can perceive even a vestige and a glint of this light and clarity in my "document," as grateful as if he had riddled out my best effort.

Munich, July 1925   Klaus Mann

THE PIOUS DANCE

PROLOGUE

I SEE a hotel room in some small town in Southern Europe and in it a young man sits writing a letter—but I do not know to whom. He has moved his desk next to the window. It is getting on for evening. The writer is making use of the last of the day, the last glimmer of light.

There is a small balcony beyond the window and then come trees. But behind and between the treetops, which stand out black against the transparent silver of the sky, the sea shimmers in its whiteness. It can barely be seen, but one can feel its nearness, its breathing, its moving and powerful drowsiness.

Before the stark silver of the not-quite evening sky, the face of the young writer is outlined in dead black like a snipped silhouette. His nose juts out somewhat sharply, his hair falls dark and lank over his forehead. His eyes, deeply hooded in a kind of distrait gentleness, look beyond the note paper that lies white and unfolded before him to a few photographs in simple frames which are arranged with remarkable symmetry at the back of the desk.

One cannot quite make out what the photographs represent, because it is too dark.

But the young man turns in his hotel chair and looks around the room behind him. Right beside the bed on the night table there stands yet a fourth photograph, but this one cannot be clearly distinguished in the twilight either. Is it a child or a boy or is it a young man? Movingly earnest and calm, it stares into the blurring space the way children do when someone is telling them something important. But, so far as one can still see, a black rosary has been placed around the photograph. Otherwise it is now so dark in the room that one can no longer say whether the man at the desk is looking at the picture with the rosary or only at the large bed that, white, silent, piled high with pillows, stately and full of mystery, seems to be waiting for something.—His gaze can no longer be traced, it is lost in the room.

But he soon turns back to the sheet of paper and starts writing again. Apparently he began this letter a long time ago, in a different ink, perhaps in a different city as well. But now he continues. Eagerly, rapidly, and yet a bit awkwardly, his hand moves over the paper. His words line up, big as a child's letters and full of faith. And his face is bent over it, earnest and full of devotion, and yet with little smile lines around the mouth—the way children crouch over a game that is extremely important to them and yet remains a game.—Once his gaze even slips off the paper and over to one of the photographs in front of him. Then it seems as if a quiet voice is speaking to him, clearly, gently and yet sternly: "My dear boy, whatever are you writing at, what is that highstrung narrative? Pathetic and lunatic at the same time?"—And the young man, with the understandable arrogance of youth, replies with his mysterious, comically cunning look of a child at play, "Go on wondering— she to whom I am writing will understand. Today I am closer to her than to you. My words are always crazy, my words are confused. But beyond the words things will be clear, there is clarity beyond the good old words."—And then he bends his unwrinkled brow and devoutly goes on writing.

But suddenly he jumps up, steps away from the desk and stands in the middle of the room. He stretches out his arms as if he wants to embrace something. But it turns out that he is merely stretching, as if just aroused from sleep. For he is surrounded by a room, a small dusky hotel room—and on the wall in a bright wooden frame hangs a small painting of a lady and a prancing horse. And there stands a bed, silent, piled high—what has it experienced?—And outside, in a foreign hallway, the chambermaids stand around and chat. And a vague foreign scent wafts through the window—how flowers thrive in the South!—And faces stare blurrily from the desk. The one by the bedside, gazing with such moving earnestness and composure—is it a child, a boy or a young man? But someone has adorned him with a black rosary. And a half-finished letter, a white letter, lies there, the words lined up boldly and full of faith.

Outside there is a foreign southern city, basking in the evening warmth, its fountains plashing noisily. And then comes the sea.

He drops his arms; with his arms at his side he looks slender, narrow and disciplined. That way he looks like a pious young soldier, whose face pales above the black of his jacket in this twilight—standing sentry duty for something holy, acting the sentinel in this foreign room, across this foreign sea, across this foreign world.

ONE

1

ONE night, when Andreas Magnus was still living in his father's house, he had a dream. But this dream was so painful, so unusually traumatic that when Andreas awoke from it, he found his pillowcase bathed in tears.

The dream began in a small dim stall, filled from top to bottom with crosses and tapers, all sorts of holy objects of silver and wax. Among these, very indistinct amid the many shadows, the saleswoman stood behind the counter, her hair curiously curled, as though it were divided or gathered through little bright-blue bows into a single mass, her eyes glancing stealthily with a peculiar watery green gaze. But Andreas bargained his last few coins with her over a black rosary. It cost a large sum—a disproportionately large sum, it seemed to him—and his pockets were very empty. To tell the truth, he did not feel comfortable about pushing his remaining cash across this lady's counter. But, smiling sanctimoniously, she gently took the money. Nimbly she concealed it in a black leather bag, no doubt intended for benevolent purposes.— Then as he was preparing to leave the shop, she quietly bade him farewell with a "God keep you," the way people say it to children setting off on a long journey.

The place must have smelled of incense and closeness, he now noticed for the first time. Outside the air was so pure and clear. Apparently he was on a hill overlooking a big city. But he did not recognize the city, for it was as blurred and formless as water at his feet on a dark night. Behind him, a little higher up, a white church gleamed, arching loftily in the night.— Andreas walked a little farther, holding the rosary. The white road ran before him like a purling stream, downhill towards the city that buzzed and roared in the distance. On the way he wound the chaplet twice round his hand—how cool the beads were on his flesh. No wonder it had been so expensive.— Suddenly he asked himself whether the saleswoman with the bows in her hair might not have been a bit of an angel, an angel with a vacuous, pious and mysterious look, who might now and then play music beside the Madonna. Andreas thought it not impossible that an angel had pocketed his money and serenely put it away in a black bag. For what might not happen in the vicinity of so white a church? What miracle was inconceivable—the wanderer asked himself—above this city?

A woman sat by the side of the road. Andreas saw her from afar. She sat like one who has wearily encamped beside a body of water and now, silently, mind a blank, watches the current flow.—Then, as he stopped by her, he suddenly recognized who she was. Amid the stiff, yet beautiful folds of her dark mantle she sat as amid ringing gold and precious jewels. And yet, gray and thin, she was as homely as any woman by the roadside. Amid the black cloth of her dress her hands hung as wearily as if she had been doing good deeds all day and had handled much.

Andreas recognized her. But he did not dare, even in silence, to put a name to her. All words which might denote her and the other prayers that had been devised for her seemed too petty and also too pompous to suit her most loving kindness. And so he wanted to find a new name for her, a new formulation for her holiness, the most devout of sounds.—But nothing occurred to him.

So he stood before her, and yet knew no word for her whom he would have done homage; so he held out to her his rosary, the one he had bought with his last remaining coins. He offered it to her—but the Mother of God merely shook her head. And suddenly Andreas realized: she does not want the gift. He realized why she was shaking her head: she wanted no offering of his.

He let the chaplet fall to the ground—clicking a bit like a wounded garter snake, it coiled up on the white road. "Why don't you want it?" he asked quietly. And the mother's voice—small and silvery like the voice of Andreas's sister Marie Thérèse—answered: "Not yet. You have not yet earned it. You have not yet suffered for it. You have never yet understood me. You are still young and full of pride. You must first have experienced the great thing, before I deign to accept your homage. Have you ever understood me? Never yet—."

But as she spoke, she vanished even farther from his sight. Her slender body in its mantle was gliding away into the far distance. Only her last words hung behind strangely, like a silver cloud in the dark air:

"Never yet—."

Andreas wanted to stoop down and pick up the rosary, but then he lacked the courage and stood upright.

The bells of the white church tolled their chime over the unknown city in the distance. Their powerful tones mingled with Mary's low, fading, last words that moved away like curling smoke. The bells' song provided a clangorous, ostentatious background for this woeful lament: "Never yet—never yet—"

Andreas looked up to see the stars. There were none to be

seen, the night was cloudy and overcast. Only the city made a noise, warning, almost imperious, like a body of water rising and coming ever closer.

At that Andreas woke up to find he had wept in his sleep. He stretched out in bed and tasted his salty tears. He tried to reach for his rosary, he thought he must have left it on the night table beside him. But he could not find it. His hands groped about and, without having found the cool beads, he lay back on his pillows.

2

It was late morning when he first awoke. He raised his head, propped it on his hands and looked around. This was his room, this was where he had grown up. Wasn't he at home here?—There was his furniture, the walls he had known for years. With his head propped up, he looked around the room and it seemed like something one has seen for a long time and never understood and then suddenly looks almost terrifying. That was what his surroundings were like—so clearly, so wonderfully strange and familiar.

There he lay in the center of it all, and brooded. There were the books he loved, piled in little heaps, standing in long rows. Scandinavian books and French books and German books. All sorrow become form, passion become lyricism, life's excitement become rhythm, love's grief become sound.—And there were pictures too, photographs and reproductions of the great painter Frank Bischof, who was a friend of his father's. They looked so sharp and clear against their dark backgrounds.—And there, on the other side, in front of the wardrobe, lay crazy piles of his own sketches, tossed together pell-mell. He could not go on looking, and turned his head away. Dancing bodies and jagged landscapes and disgusting caricatures—the grossness and grotesquerie of a budding naturalism side by side with a fragile, timid romanticism.

9

Blatant documents, leftovers, experiments in creativity from his uncertain, ever groping, ever passionately exploring youth—touching and painful for the one who had evolved them only a very short time after their inception. But close to this bunch of sketches and beginnings stood the homely framed photograph of a late Gothic Madonna, half turned away amid the devoutly artificial drapery folds of her garments, as if all this lay at her feet. But the gesture with which she caught up her mantle, the expression with which she turned away her glorious head, were not those of one who accepts, but of one who virtually rejects.

Then Andreas felt that he understood his dream. Thought, like a sorrow or a sickness, rose up in him. He laid his head back again and closed his eyes.—She would not accept his offering, with a loving denial of grace she had spurned what he longed to bring her. All the others who had served her, whose books and pictures lay around, each had served her with his skill. Some mundanely, some spiritually, some in scorn and anguish, others in humility and silence. Each one had laid his song at her feet—the song of his life. But he did not have one yet. Its beginnings were all over the place, its efforts and preludes were everywhere. But he had not yet found the tune— he and his generation.

Suddenly bolt upright in bed, roused to indignation like one who has had a vision, his brows knit in thought, he saw what lay before him, and how it compassed him round. With an almost frighteningly sudden urgency and penetrating clarity he grasped the situation. This was how things stood— this was his environment. Like a powerful and violent simplification, everything became clear to him.

The fathers' generation had done its part and would go on doing it in future and develop further. It had grown great in worth and deeds or in torment and distress—but it had grown great, it had done it by itself, it had found its means of expression.—And then came the ghastly dividing line, the bloody conflagration, the fiery departure, then came the war and the great all-consuming upheaval. He had been born into this war—he, Andreas Magnus, the individual who stood before him in his erstwhile perplexity, although he realized in his heart of hearts that this perplexity must be indigenous to a generation, an entire species, and not peculiar to one individual. His dull, dreamy childhood has been spent thus during the revolutionary days of 1914, whose grandeur, whose mighty pathos he was still unable to understand, but which had stamped itself on his soul only as a kind of great uprising, a clanking, booming noise, a vague period after which everything had to be different from what it was before, and had reshaped his soul. And the background, the environment for the years of his earliest awareness, his earliest perception, learning—in short, the years between eleven and thirteen had been that other tentative, yet dangerous revolution, that desperate upheaval that might well destroy what was old and mature but could not give birth to anything new out of its internal turmoil—the revolution of 1918.

The previous generation—he was sure of it now—, the species that had reached some forty years of age the very day the war began, had also come to know disturbance and unwonted confusion during this catastrophe. It too had been overwhelmed by the great commotion, and many who thought themselves prepared and mature had to relearn, inwardly and outwardly, in the midst of peril. But even then, they had only to relearn something that already existed, to transform it as far as possible into something else that the times, with supreme inexorability, demanded.—How much worse, yes, how much more desperate it was for those who had for the first time to find something amid the chaos, to discover for the first time their own tone amid this dissonant clamor of tones, find their way past all the extremities in which they were placed.

Andreas sat rigidly in bed for several minutes. Never yet had he realized all this so clearly, so very, very clearly: that he still had no path, still had no tune—and yet signposts were erected for him on so many corners, enticing him to choose the direction their beatific dogma indicated.

But downstairs in his study sat his father, his dear father. He was no privileged person, simply an honest, clever middle-class man, a doctor years ago, passably able and now long retired. He knew what he wanted. At first the upheaval had disconcerted him too, but he had found his way out of it and, somewhat altered, was back on the road that seemed to suit him. His scholarly work flourished, splendidly, so it seemed. And his friendship with the great painter Frank Bischof gave his life a greater meaning and surely constituted its most distinguished virtue. Perhaps "friendship" is too portentous a word to describe this relationship. His father and Frank Bischof had known one another from their youth. And the painter often bestowed the honor of his visits on him.

But the son, after bitterly mournful dreams, had to wake up suddenly, sit bolt upright and knit his brows, as in terror, as if he wanted to appear serious—only because his situation appeared before him in its alarming vagueness.—Thus his youth, the youth which had begun amid the clamor of the revolution, had become blotchy and disorganized, blemished and impure, though innocent, for it longed regretfully for purity, clarity and light. Careening from one attraction to another, or surrendering in confusion to all at once—amusing and painful at the same time.—It had gone astray and its helpless search for direction had become childish—quixotically corrupted on every street. Gone to the bad in merriment and pain. He had already given skeptical consideration to revolutionary gestures, the deep abyss between what had gone before was already obvious to him, but he preferred to renounce the attractive charms of revolution or use them only occasionally, as a mask and a last resort. Previously one had been glad if a resting place had offered itself, a straight line one could cleave to. Of course, one had often been frivolous and inclined to joke, as if the most trivial things on earth were there for the first time and presumably the truly important things would never be there again—frivolous in a radically extravagant way, which seemed to deny anything serious, distorted the values of things, played catch with the basic essentials.—But more often, one had yielded to sorrow, a cruel hopelessness, which was irresistible and provided no more meaning or perception than that everything was over and nothing more was to be done and the end was now and the only reason this whole questionable postwar generation was born, the only reason God dreamed it up was to frame the yawning gulf of this decline—a useless ornament on the great annihilation, an already extinct species.

It was not his fault and it was not his father's fault. It was nobody's fault. But that was how everything was.—His father would have liked to help and said, "You see, my son, we all had to go through it once—that's puberty—that's a difficult time for young people—." And then the son had looked at the floor and made no reply and did not say that it was something else, not the psychic and physical crisis of adolescence, but a danger, a rift of a deeper, more trenchant, more fatal kind.— He lived with his father and told him nothing. His beloved mother was dead. Her portrait, filled with care and kindness, stared critically, exhortingly, observantly from all the dressers. "Our parents are good," Andreas thought suddenly. "They have been so good to us.—But they cannot help. They stare full of care, as if looking at pictures, but their gaze never reaches us."

He lay back on the pillows. His hands kept stroking the pillows—as if they were trying to smooth something down. But all he thought as he did this was: Just now the Mother of

God would not accept the rosary—did not accept the little offering—did not find me worthy after all I've suffered.—Or had he not suffered the essential thing? Does the essential thing still lie before him?—What about the picture he had been toiling over for weeks? Was that inessential too? The big picture on which he placed such great, uncommon hopes, that it might at last be the shaping, the formulation, the declaration of faith of these past years? Would she also reject this offering with the aloof, immutable grace of her gesture of repudiation?

He closed his eyes and fervently conjured up the picture, let its bright, almost glowing colors and passionate, distorted contours rise before him. It stood in the next room, half finished on its wooden easel: the Lord God with little children dancing around Him. How bright was the little red wall in front of which they appeared in relief. And behind the wall how golden and blue, shimmering and bathed in holy evening light the mountain range rose in quaint peaks. The little wall seemed to be spattered with blood, the bright red blood of children.— The children's movements were certainly strangely hampered, their dance was stiff and cramped as if they were dancing in agony. Marie Thérèse danced more gracefully.—His children had earnest faces above their gaudy smocks, earnest and ecstatic. These faces did not breathe, barely lived. They were like pious and yet facetious masks, motley painted masks of glass.—The countenance of God Himself did not stand out of the darkness much, that needed working on the next time. But it had already begun to take on shape and expression out of the surrounding haze, the big face of the old man with the grizzled beard and the unnaturally round eyes, fixed, empty, yet filled with great knowledge. That's how it should be, that's how God's countenance ought to be: fixed and empty and yet filled with great knowledge, the way a well full of darkness is. Cruelly and untouchably hedged round by the black beard, the mouth bleeding in its thicket, but the eyes filled with knowledge of all afflictions—and to know is to sympathize and be indulgent.

The young painter Andreas smiled in his bed in a kind of private joy. That's how the picture would be: children are dancing an ecstatic and ungainly dance in front of a low blood-spattered wall. In the middle God's face emerges from the darkness: fixed, empty and yet indulgent. And way at the back the mountains would be watered with blue gold. That would be his picture and the "essential" thing.—

Then he thought he must get up, he had lain abed long enough, and sprang out of bed in his hasty resolve.—All at once, as soon as he had left the bed, he walked barefoot and with unkempt hair through the room, suddenly sobered by the cold of day. He had determined on the mirror as his goal. A far distance.—He proceeded barefoot over the red floor, as if it were hot sand. He lifted his feet curiously, like a cautious pedestrian. Barefoot he stood before the mirror. He looked at himself a long time—deadly earnest at the start. He knit his brows, he dealt out earnest reproaches to the sleep-intoxicated pilgrim in the white nightshirt before him. "Yes, yes," he said sternly, as if at a timid eavesdropper wagging his finger, "you learned something last night, you learned how far you've got with all your confusion. And now you want to paint a goddam God, of all things, and masks of children dancing around. Well, we'll see—"

But suddenly he smiled—and did not know why. The smile took complete possession of him, engulfed him. "So that's what I am," he thought, smiling. "So young, so fourteen-year-old young. My hair so tangled, my nightshirt so short, my feet so bare."—Had his childhood been restless and soiled?—Ah, but today he looked so pure in the mirror. Was it worth going through even more? And what if the thing that stood half-finished in the next room were not the "essential thing" either? Did everything still lie before him?—That's how it might turn out.

And suddenly, laughing in high spirits, he pulled off his nightshirt and stretched, naked. He twisted a bathtowel round his waist, laughing with conceit, draping it decoratively as if it were a silk garment. This way he looked like a Greek youth at the gymnasium—and if he draped it the other way, he looked just like a young monk.

Laughing he ran down the corridor to the bathroom. "So young," he kept thinking as he ran, "so very young."

3

It was rather late by the time he came down to breakfast—a little after eleven. Marie Thérèse was already back from school—yes, she had lessons from nine to eleven. Chirping and chattering, she ran right up to him at the foot of the stairs, and he had to carry her into the dining-room. Her friend Peter was there, she reported hurriedly,—and the word "friend" was touching and much too big for her bright little voice. How thoroughly small she was, how incredibly fairy-tale small she lay in Andreas's arms. Her little face, framed with fine auburn hair, smooth as spun silk, lay close to his, and she had entwined her arms around his neck, so as not to fall off. And her little face was sweet and funny. Her mouth was a little too big and gap-toothed as well—almost all her teeth had fallen out, which gave her a touching, yet droll look. But while her mouth related all her adventures on the way to school, her glistening brown eyes spoke their own clever and innocent dialogue.

Peterchen was already sitting in the dining room and politely stood up to greet his friend's big brother. "Good morning," he said and bowed and held out his small, rather damp hand. He was wearing his striped sailor's suit, and his hair, which he wore cropped, as did Marie Thérèse, was always a bit unkempt and sticky. He too was small, barely as big as his lady—nor had he many more teeth: a small, toothless cavalier. But a cavalier all the same, bold, polite and bright-eyed. "Good morning," he said, and bowed.—Marie Thérèse in her pinafore stood roguishly to one side.

Andreas drank tea, while the children took far too much bread-and-butter in both hands, making it difficult for them to bite into it. Meanwhile they talked with their mouths full about Fräulein Amtmann, their teacher, and how she had presented them with cough-drops, at which Andreas nodded absentmindedly. And had he forgot, Marie Thérèse asked and winked roguishly, that their Herr Papa was celebrating his birthday—his fifty-first—today.—Andreas winked back. For—yes—he actually had forgot.

They left hurriedly and ran across the terrace and down into the garden. They made a small couple on the greensward— a small, sweet, running couple. Marie Thérèse turned her head once and laughed back at her brother, eating alone at the table and watching them. Now far off in the greenery, she turned her face to him, and her shimmering eyes spoke out of it. "Won't you come?" her high, delicate, tempting little voice called. But her brother only shook his head.

Slowly he stood up. Now he had work to do.

In the vestibule he ran into his father. In his camel's-hair dressing gown he came out of the study where, every day until this time, he set himself to write a little, some short passage for a specialized work of scholarship that was making progress ever so slowly and was now drawing to an end. He would head upstairs where an elderly barber's assistant was waiting to give him his daily shave. Then he would go for a walk.

Andreas stood still for a moment. "Good morning," he said and looked at the floor. He almost never looked at his father. "Good morning—off for your walk now? I really almost forgot that today was your birthday. Congratulations.—" And he smiled a polite, fleeting smile. But although this politeness could not be called cordial, it could not exactly be termed cold. A certain submissiveness, yes, something approaching a melancholy and covert veneration flickered in it, instantly lending sincerity to his demeanor which at first sight seemed cool and aloof.

"Thanks, thanks," his father replied, with a cigar in his mouth. Then, allowing his gaze to glide through the lenses of his spectacles and out the window, "The weather's turned fine. This morning it looked as if it were almost going to rain."

"Yes, but it's still cloudy," said Andreas and started up the stairs. That was the extent of their conversation.

His father looked after him. There goes his son.—He had work to do upstairs. But the father had doubts about his talent. It was a fact that Frank Bischof almost seemed to dismiss his studies and first drafts utterly. Dismiss, the father considered, standing in the middle of the vestibule in his dressing gown, is perhaps too harsh a word. He was accustomed to regard them with a smile as something contemptible and almost deserving of pity. "Yes, yes," the smile seemed to say, "there's not much there—."

There goes his son, a slim figure walking upstairs, like someone who is always moving away. And there he stood, the father.—But suddenly he thought—and he clasped his hands as affection bubbled up warmly in him: "Marie Thérèse will be better off. Things have been a bit peculiar with him, I really don't understand him very well, I can't tell where his path is leading. But Marie Thérèse is my child.—" And, hands still clasped, he went upstairs as well, but much more slowly than his son had, one step at a time.—

Now Andreas sat before the big picture. His hands lay slackly in his lap, as idly as if they could never pick up a brush again. Yes—work—paint—prepare—

God's face was still rather blotchy, the children's figures loosely delineated and motley. So, on with the work—the sky was not transparent enough, the blue was still too crude, it has to be like glass.—But his hands were weary and made no move.

That morning he had been laughing in front of the mirror, his heart had been in a kind of frenzy. But where was his great courage now?—Like a constant, gnawing, unbearable torment, one thought filled his mind, his whole body: So many have found means of expression and have depicted their heart's suffering and joy. I won't be able to. I won't know what's wrong, but I won't be able to. With what relentless severity the planets must have been aligned at the hour of my birth. How cruel, how incomprehensibly cruel it was of God to endow a man with the irrepressible passion to create a work of art and to have him grow up and live in such unavoidably difficult conditions that he has not the strength to carry it out. And so he sat before his easel.

Everything that the morning had shown him in such terrifying clarity, he now perceived as a suffocating agony, an almost crippling grief—as he confronted his work. Sitting before the easel, he bowed his head deeply. He felt as if he would never be able to raise it again. He was so disgusted with his hands—he would not lift them and create with them. The other fellow—he'd been able to do it—Frank Bischof had been able to do it. Nowadays he was revered, and his heart was content. Content, thought Andreas in a kind of impotent rage, now he's content.—And he conjured up his face, that long, narrow face with the hooked nose, the rather long upper lip, handsomely framed by a grizzled, trimmed moustache and goatee, the eyes somewhat hooded but still shining with a light that poor Andreas facing his picture could not understand. All he thought was—and did not stir from his chair though his mouth quivered a bit as if he had tasted something bitter—: so now he's a paragon, now he's the standard. Once he too must have been impassioned, divided, troubled and full of doubt.

But he had found himself.—And he overlooked the still, deeply engraved lines of pain that lay around his eyes and narrow closed mouth of that face. He could not see them at all.

But almost every single picture by Frank Bischof rose up before him. The "Councilor in Black" and the "Lady on the Promenade" and "Portrait of His Mother." The pictures from his earliest period stood before him, they were so badly done, gloomy and sarcastic. But then his work matured, developing into ever stronger, more human and at the same time more severe forms. His latest painting—and perhaps his greatest—how brown and darkly clear it was, dignified in its earnestness, yes, acerbic in the sharp outlines and yet so mature, so exquisitely humorous in its way.—Spitefully and with veneration the man with the unskilled hands reproached himself with it.

And so he sat.—And what if these efforts miscarried too? What if once again nothing that he had yearned for weeks to instill in this composition, yearned to give form to breathed and lived in it?

But suddenly he closed his eyes which had been lost in the twilight landscape of the unfinished picture, closed them so tightly it almost hurt. Yes—what if this too miscarried—. He thought no thoughts, nothing specific, nothing sharply defined. But somehow he knew why so blessed and so fleeting a smile settled around his brushstrokes.—He would make everything depend on that.

Through the open window the wind wafted the faint cries of the children playing in the autumn garden: Marie Thérèse and her squire. So Andreas walked to the window. He saw his little sister squatting in a pile of yellow leaves in the middle of the lawn, her delicate, yet rather dirty hands before her face. Peter was running around her in a circle and reciting, almost chanting, a poem.—Such was their game.

Andreas called out something to them. Then Marie

Thérèse took her hands from her face and laughed at him. Peter halted in his circular track—he stood in the middle of the grass with his legs apart, in his tight sailor suit, his hair plastered down and both hands balled into fists in his pockets.—Marie Thérèse had taken off her white pinafore. She squatted on the lawn in a blood-red smock. The sun shone directly into their faces. They blinked at the sun.

At the window Andreas thought about the children and the Good Lord rebuked him with them. But then he suddenly realized that Frank Bischof would be having dinner with them that evening, at the fifty-first birthday party.—And his daughter with him. Ursula Bischof was coming today.

And as he spoke and laughed down to the children, he decided to show her his big picture today, his picture of the bearded God. Ursula would tell him how much she liked his picture.

4

Peterchen and Marie Thérèse sat as before at the dinner table. They had had big white napkins tied round them and were teasing one another with nudges and pinches at the lower end of the table, while the maid, an acidulous spinster, ladled eight servings of soup into bowls. Peterchen's sticky hair was now brushed very flat—it seemed almost as delicately silken as Marie Thérèse's—and they both had clean hands; somewhat scratched from playing in the bushes, but otherwise dainty, they lay on the tablecloth.

The spinster maid had crowned the Doctor's chair with small, hard red blossoms, in honor of the birthday party. Now she went around with her pointed nose and plopped a little dumpling into every bowl, so that the broth splashed slightly.— Then she rapped at the door to the next room and with a curtsey bade the company come to the table.

They came in, a chattering group: Frank Bischof, his

daughter Ursula, Dr. Magnus and his elder sister. As they were taking their seats, the sister, the widowed Baroness Geldern, asked Frank Bischof solicitously and inquisitively: "I have so many times wanted to ask you, Master, why you never take the opportunity now and again to refute or rather simply controvert the attacks made on you so frequently by the more shameless of the younger literati and art critics."—

Frank Bischof replied in a very soft, very muffled voice, as he smiled gently, almost mournfully, behind his grizzled beard. "Why should I defend myself?" was all he said—and did not interrupt the progress of his soup spoon.

"You may be right." Still Widow Geldern remonstrated, "I insist, Master," she cried and stared in shock at the ceiling as she replaced her bowl on its plate, "but I insist—." Ursula's gaze rested directly on her father who was eating with his face bent over the table. Her eyes were very black, with a slight glint of red in them.

Andreas was a bit tardy in walking into the room. He blushed a bit as he excused himself to Frank Bischof, the aunt and Ursula. His seat was at the corner, between Ursula and Marie Thérèse. With a passing and uneasy fondness, he stroked Marie Thérèse's hair. Then he began to eat hurriedly. But his sister roguishly threatened him and said that he really should not get any food, whereupon Peterchen giggled brightly behind his enormous napkin. Doctor Magnus laughed quite heartily and as he laughed raised his glass to toast his little daughter. "Your health!" he said and nodded.

It was an intimate, but really splendid little banquet. The food in particular was a great success, each course served acidulously but decorously by the spinster maid. The widowed Baroness, who had once lived in comfortable, one might say almost magnificent circumstances and who had the surprised expression of a princess who could not grasp why everything was now so different, spoke a bit too preciously and profusely, but not without a certain touching and yellowing primness. Yellowish lace crackled all over her cheap black taffeta dress, her somewhat graying hair was artfully curled and waved. Small pearls shimmered around her scrawny neck.

She pressed her narrow lips together and said ornamentally, "Perhaps it is retrograde on our part not to have learned to appreciate that ugly art is better than beautiful art. I cannot get it into my head," she confessed and smiled wanly, "that Gustav Mahler is supposed to be more worthwhile than my Mendelssohn-Bartholdy."—

Frank Bischof chose to keep his narrow face bent over his plate. Rarely did he let his gray eyes, knowing, yet not hard, fall on his interlocutor. His only answer to all these questions was rather formulaic, precise and gentle. "Who is to determine what is beautiful?" he asked doubtfully and suddenly raised his eyes to Frau von Geldern's faded face, whose white, excessively delicate oval still had a certain attenuated charm. "I never flattered myself that I created anything truly beautiful," the graybeard added, mildly and almost to himself.

"But you have created it for all of us!" the widowed Baroness declared smartly and raised her hands so that the lace appliqué crackled. "You are the great exponent, the great representative of our generation, the bourgeois era!" Her pale countenance had grown flushed, a hectic red mounted to her cheekbones.—

But he, the great painter, whom an entire race had acknowledged and celebrated as its representative, suddenly turned his head away; he gazed out into space, into vagueness, and a silent laugh played about his mouth. "Who knows what is to come?" was all he said and he shook his head.—

Then a fear came over Andreas and a profound wonder gripped his heart. So that question was in Bischof's mind as well as in his own.—Ursula's serene gaze traveled silently between the two of them, inquiring back and forth between

Andreas and her father. But they both sat with downcast faces.

After the roast Frank Bischof tapped on his glass and delivered a short after-dinner speech. "My dear friend," he said and turned his long face to Dr. Magnus, as he spoke quietly but fastidiously with the most precise enunciation of his final syllables, "a year ago today, when you had reached your fiftieth birthday I spoke in your honor. But when I think back to the many times, on occasions both festive and solemn, when you made a toast in my honor, it almost strikes me that we are both forgotten old gentlemen who have nothing better to do than mutually celebrate one another, just to be sure of being celebrated." Frank Bischof smiled, but his daughter's dark gaze rested on this smile. So much self-deprecation on the part of a world-famous man made the Widow Geldern shudder with amusement and nod her head, while Andreas listened without looking up. "Dear friend," the speaker went on quietly, "we shall not disavow the affection of the young who are near and dear to us, today we shall not disavow our children. But there is such a distance between them and us, and youth still has a long way to go. Both parties may yet have much to achieve in the way of adaptation and self-understanding: the day will come when they will disavow us all. Then perhaps it may be that only a couple of old men will still understand one another, however much they may be misconstrued in this wide world.—We have so much in common, even our first love, the girl next door, and our mothers gossiped together over their shopping. Even our dear wives, whom God has called to Him, were joined in intimate friendship. And if nothing else were to bind us, for their sakes alone we could never forget one another.—I will speak at your sixtieth birthday too, Georg Paul, and if I am very wrinkled and absent-minded, you shall raise a wineglass at my eightieth." He clinked glasses all round with a look of affection.

Amid all the cordial confusion Andreas thought only: He

called him by his first name—how odd—he had addressed him as Georg Paul.—

His father's eyes had grown moist. Over and over again he called to Marie Thérèse across the table: "Did you understand all of that, my dear child? Did you understand it properly?" And Marie Thérèse smiled at him with shining eyes. Peterchen too, nearly suffocated by the large napkin, had assumed a grave expression and looked startled. The gentleman had spoken so wonderfully, so quietly and sadly, and yet with a smile.—

Meanwhile the Widow Geldern clapped her fragile upraised hands as at the theatre. "How charming!" she kept whispering, "No, no—how moving!" And dress and lace appliqué quietly crackled.—But now came the cake.

Afterwards, over coffee and cigarettes, Dr. Magnus was merry and in high spirits. He sat festively in a frock coat with a cigar in his mouth and told extended anecdotes which, though somewhat long-winded and pointless, provoked general mirth. "Fritz and Kurt, two honest-to-goodness Dresden tramps," he began in a rather dubious Saxon dialect, and his elder sister laughed as brightly as a young girl, although her narrow mouth trembled so much that she had to cover it with her pocketbook.

Suddenly the father felt like dancing. Marie Thérèse was riding on his knee as he shook her to the rhythm of a lively tune, when he asked his sister to play them a waltz on the piano, he wanted to ask Fräulein Ursula for a dance— Fräulein Ursula was sitting silently, blowing cigarette smoke in the air, as if it were a game like blowing soap bubbles. But when her father's friend asked her to dance, she said that would be nice and stood up at once.

He took her roguishly by the arm and led her across the floor, while the Baroness, her head tilted to one side, presided at the piano.—A little stiff in the legs, the Doctor whirled

Ursula over the carpet, but she danced beautifully, her head tossed back a bit. It really was rather strenuous for him, and little beads of sweat stood out on his forehead. But still he smiled.

Frank Bischof and Andreas stood against the wall looking on. Once the father turned to the young man by his side. "What are you working on now, may I ask?" he said and for a moment his clever eyes moved to Andreas's face. But all Andreas felt was suffocated rage. "Why doesn't he call me young man straight out?" he thought and clenched his teeth. He only replied, "Oh—nothing special—," and looked down at his shoes. Then the Master turned his gaze away from him as well.—Frank Bischof stared at the dancing couple, but Andreas glared darkly and defiantly at the floor. He was dressed unconventionally in a blue shirt with Russian embroidery, buttoned up to his chin.—His face topped it, smooth and yet twisted in anger. "Might just as well have called me 'young man'!" he thought to the floorboards.—At the piano the widow's urgent, slender hands played of Vienna and the blue Danube.

Later Ursula said to her father, whom the Baroness was preciously and circumstantially telling about her reduced circumstances, "You know, you have to dance a shimmy with me tonight, Dr. Magnus hasn't seen anything of the brilliant way I've taught you." This time Andreas had to stand in as musician, for Baroness Geldern, in accordance with her principles and capabilities, had to be excused from playing a shimmy. Therefore Andreas sat at the keyboard like a member of a Russian orchestra; his hair fell over his forehead and he played freely, as if passionately enthusiastic. The keys lamented beneath his fingers in dull rhythm, it was a shimmy of the ponderous, martially melancholy sort. But then a melody came sweeping in, lighthearted and childlike, in contrast to the harsh one, frisking airily along. It cooed and tittered to the bass, which groaned in time like a tramping horse.

Once while playing Andreas turned around. Ursula was dancing with her father.—He hoped he would see the Master making a sorry laughingstock of himself in an effort at modern dance. But he skipped over the carpet with a certain charm if also some anxiety; indeed his eyes were filled with anguish. His daughter smiled in his arms. She was wearing a wonderful white dress, Andreas noticed for the first time, studded from top to bottom with little pearls that clicked quietly in the dance.

Baroness Geldern said from her little easy chair: "I must confess I am surprised that Frank Bischof can be a party to such nigger dancing. He of all people, the representative of our generation." But Dr. Magnus only grinned.—Peterchen and Marie Thérèse stood in the doorway and observed earnestly and reverently.—

Afterwards as Ursula was sitting down again in a big armchair, Andreas said behind her, "Would you care to come upstairs with me? I'd very much like to show you something—"

As they walked up the stairs beside one another, Ursula remarked quietly, taking a few steps ahead so that he could not see her face, "I've seen so little of you lately."—But behind her Andreas's voice merely replied, "I've been working."—They used to be together almost every day.

Downstairs the Baroness was unfolding the sad tale of her life to the gentlemen. "My little daughter Elsbeth is now employed as a typist," she reported dolefully, "and naturally her boss gives her a terrible time."

There was a slight twitch around her thin mouth and her poor neck, where pearls shimmered as a token of erstwhile pomp, and in her anguished eyes shone the agony of a whole extinct class.

*

He opened the door to the bright, bare room in which he worked. He hesitated for a moment before turning on the light, as if he were afraid. They stood next to one another in the dark by the door, but not so close that anything but their hands could touch.

Then it was bright. Dazzled they blinked in the white light that suddenly filled the room with a seemingly malevolent quaver and flicker. The picture stood almost directly beneath the glare of the electric bulb, a light that was merciless and unbecoming to it—and all Andreas could think was, "Who stuck it there?" With a curt gesture of invitation he pointed toward it, but she ignored his movement which was both arrogant and tentative. She stood still and looked.

Andreas thought: Only women can stare like that. The head bent that way, yielding totally and offering no opposition to seeing and accepting. That's a woman standing there, he thought suddenly, and was as glad as if he had never known her and she was now meeting him for the first time and "is looking at what I've been working on. That's the way she looks at it: her head jutting forward a bit, her hair black, very black, but with red, never blue highlights, and her eyes the same: black with a reddish glint. And her name is Ursula. That's how she stands, a little stiff, almost wooden maybe—stands and stares—."

She turned her face back to him, but no smile played about her mouth. She stood in the middle of the circle of light in her white dress and stared at the easel with knit brows. "Now she'll say something," Andreas implored inwardly, "now she'll be specific, I do so much count on it. She knows so much as she stands there," he thought in confusion, "she knows it not with her head but with her body, as she stands there like that. She knows it with her voice, I can learn everything from her voice, even if she says something irrelevant to the subject—" And he could no longer endure simply standing beneath the weight of the silence, he walked across the room and sat down heavily before the little piano at the back, pushed, brown and inconspicuous, against the wall, waiting for him the way a homely little nanny waits for her spoiled and troublesome charge.

Then the girl before the easel uttered the first word—it fell stinging and harsh, as the first raindrops drip down the trees on to the earth when the air has long been sultry and still before the storm. "Yes," said the girl, "yes—but can anyone believe it?" And her countenance, whose smile was so gentle and doubtful and alien that one dare not address it, turned back to the picture itself. "If anyone really can find something there to believe in," she said to the picture—and she searched for each word and found it the way a person stoops to pick a berry, "then what he sees in it will make him hard and pious."

Over by the piano, he began to speak with childish vehemence and childish audacity, rhetorically and confused. "You are severe," he said and his eyes filled with tears, "your verdict is against me. The things that make a man hard and pious can come only from clarity.—You know that. Your father, yes, I really believe that all his life he created things people could believe in." And his face—an eighteen-year-old face with its tearful eyes and oppressed brow—digressed further into agonized spitefulness. "Nevertheless," he went on and suddenly pointed his finger at the picture, which, artificially and intricately garish, seemed to overhear his words, "nevertheless, you must already realize what I have against your father. What I have against him is that he was the spokesman, the representative of his time, its image-maker— but that time is over, no matter what—and I am not the spokesman for my time, my more modern, more pious, more passionate time—you know exactly what I mean—but I would like to be, I would like to become that for once. You say you don't believe in it. But you must at least believe in the effort. You are young too—" he suddenly said very gently and hardly dared look at her, she stood so still beside him.

"Yes," she said and, instead of looking at him or his picture, gazed out beyond both into space, "we are young—." And then she shrugged, as if she doubted it at the same time. "But what is our youth all about?" she asked—and he knew that now, in her stillness, she would interpret and clarify everything he had learned that morning as in a vision of anguish, for she was cleverer than he and a woman as well. "We grew up together, Andreas, we played and suffered together, without knowing where it all was leading us. Now you've suddenly caught the idea, like a fever, that you would like to change all this. Our playing was very passionate, our suffering was very pious, and we should have a more contemptible opinion of ourselves, as is only right, if we try to believe that this suffering and this playing were not a forecast and a dream of what time has in store, and what our time means.—But our younger generation, the rest of our great younger generation—what is it really after? Ah, it seems to have found such a simple way out of the confusion, that maze we misguidedly, passionately try to grope through. A little sport, a little politics and it is satisfied. Unaware of its profound inner misdirection it takes pride in becoming as shallow and dispassionate as possible. Oh, Andreas, the only constructive thing is to shape one's own sorrow, one's own ardor into an image that can be reshaped into the image of the suffering and ardor of a whole era, a whole generation. Our younger generation has no ardor at all, like a coward it disavows its sorrow and will not learn from it. What do you want to shape, Andreas? Nothing but your own isolated soul will ever speak out of your pictures and experiments, and no one will thank you for leaving them to complain—neither the older generation nor the younger."

And the boy listened to her talk, listened once more to what he had always known. But he found no escape from her words. The grief that issued from her twined itself so tightly round his heart and limbs that he could not stir.

But she, still standing in front of the easel, began to speak again. "You asked me before whether I was young," she said, "and your question implied a kind of reproach. I know. You think I would be disloyal to our dilemma and simply stand aloof from our plight because I take my father so seriously. And that is true: I love my father more than I do any younger generation which does nothing but make noise and hasn't even the courage to confront its own despair. But in his solemn loneliness my father has accomplished almost everything, perhaps my father is a hero."

She spoke like one who seldom makes speeches, simply and clearly. But she had not yet noticed that her audience was no longer listening, his face had long been turned away. Then she walked over to him—and the many pearls on her dress clicked with every step. "How can I comfort you," she said huskily behind his back. "At least I have one consolation for you. I see no way out for you, Andreas—I am nothing but a woman. Shall I say to you today: I believe you will find a way? I daren't, for the confusion is too great. But I wish it may be so, Andreas, I wish it so much—for your sake—for my sake—."

But he did not understand the sweet meaning of that "for my sake" nor did he see the look with which she stroked his hair and neck. He sat in his obstinacy and misery, in his arrogance and despair, and did not see the girl bending over him. All he had heard was, "I see no way out for you—"

Since he would not turn his face to hers, she took it gently between her hands and bent forward to see it. But unstemmed tears flowed from his tightly shut eyes, his whole face was now bathed in tears. The face she saw was one no one else could have beheld without contempt, without pushing it away in disgust. But she let her gaze rest upon it, and she spoke to him and his tears. "My dear Andreas," she said—and every word was soothing to him—"don't cry any more—it will be all right sooner or later. Are you so offended? Is it so hard?—My dear Andreas—"

And then her face lay over his: as kind as a mother's, as gentle as a lover's after the first night, as mysterious as the face of a sister.

Then he whispered close to her, he who wept in her sight, without self-control and without shame, like a child:

"My beloved bride—"

6

Very quietly Andreas set foot in little Marie Thérèse's room—he barely dared walk into it. Toys lay on the floor. Cautiously, to avoid bumping into anything, he found the way to the bed where she was sleeping, between the hobbyhorse and a little box.

Green shutters had been placed before the windows, but the night came cool and dark through the chinks, for the windows themselves were open.—Her little garments hung over a chair, her little smock, her bodice and her knitted underpants. Her shoes stood there too—tiny shoes. There she was, breathing between the pillows.

Her brother leaned over her. The deepest shame prevented him from disturbing her peaceful sleep, caressing her or saying goodbye to her. He only saw how her head had slipped off the pillow a bit and how her hair hung over her brow. And how her little hands, delicate and somewhat dirtied by the day, lay clenched near her face. And how she breathed.

Quietly he walked back out of her room, quietly down the stairs and out of the house.—They had become so small, her clothes on the chair. That was the only thing that made him feel sentimental. They had served their mistress by day, they had been big enough by far. They had served her innocently. And they waited humbly till the new day began once more and once more they could be of service to their sweet mistress.

Innocent were those clothes by day. And innocent was their peaceful night.

There was a light rain, he noticed for the first time. He had no sort of overcoat on. The rain was like a subdued rustling in the poplars which stood tall and black in this pitchy night. The road could scarcely be discerned.

But suddenly he realized which road he had to take. He had entirely forgot it, lost in thought. But he was not afraid when he thought of it again.—Of course—he had taken leave of little Marie Thérèse.—He began to move, but did not run in anguish. He walked slowly in the rain. His hair was hanging heavy and sodden, and water ran down his face.—But soon he would reach his goal. He could already hear how the waves of the river were beating on the stony bank.

Now he ran down the slope or rather he yielded to the downward pull like a rolling object. Now he stood by the river.

He felt no anxiety when he saw its black, ice-cold, even ebb and flow—he was almost overcome with wonder at it. It was as if his heart had stopped, far too weary and beyond any sensation like anxiety or real misery. The only thing he felt was that he was weary.—Why go any farther? Why exhaust himself still more? Even anxiety was an effort. Why not go home to this sweet innocence that coursed and flowed before him?

One had just grown too weak to evoke form from chaos, the form of living and the form of creating. One had just grown too weary to create a redemptive work of art out of the misery of the times and one's unique, isolated misery which were inextricably intertwined. One would do better to love the innocence of night than this vicious turmoil of the times, and what times had been more tumultuous, more dangerous, less innocent than ours?—He had groped his way a little, seeking, entangled in toil and filth, but now he let himself drop, was closing his eyes, bent his torso forward unsteadily like a drunken man, his heart was devoid of words, his mind of thoughts.—Words were now sins to him, thoughts crimes—he knew no more than that now he must be accepted graciously back into the sweet, rustling silence, his guiltless, joyous homeland which deep down he had always known was his ally, although it had sent him, its faithful knight, to so unendurably grievous a battle.—

But just at the moment when, his eyes tightly shut, his whole body now bent to the holy self-surrender, he had grown so close to the dark homeland, there seemed to be a great voice speaking to him out of this homeland. I do not believe that it spoke to him in words. But it must have posted a command before his eyes, the way one plants a banner before a soldier about to take an oath.

Andreas uttered no oath. But he straightened up directly. He released his gaze from the black, fluent silence before him, which was both innocence and temptation, a sweet temptation to innocence. And very steadily, without the least deflection, his gaze, now divorced from the darkness, stared out into another expanse which seemed to lie somewhere beyond the night. This one was full of adventure, full of pleasure and misery and danger. But his gaze, which did not flinch for a moment, for he had accepted the "command," seemed as if it were still somehow connected to the innocence of his beloved homeland by something that he did not yet know and therefore had to learn.

Slowly, step by step, he climbed back up the slope, which earlier, devoid of will, he had slipped down. Once he turned fully round and looked back at the water—very rapid, fast flowing,—and, after a small helpless gesture as after a rest, struck out into the void. But now he was smiling again, perhaps at himself and his weak vague movement.

Smiling he moved forward.

7

All night long he had arranged letters, books, little half-forgotten mementos from the dubious, sorely afflicted and yet squandered period of his life which came to an end at this hour.

The important thing now was to pack a few items of clothing, a couple of books, photographs and to write two more letters, two short sober letters of farewell.—One was addressed to his father and said only that no one should come looking for him, he would have enough money for the immediate future, would soon be doing all right in any case and remained forever his faithful son.—The sentences were clumsy, composed awkwardly, both proud and affectionate, like letters from schoolboys who abscond to America.—The other letter was to Ursula Bischof.

He put the letter to his father on the breakfast table that stood already laid in the still dark dining room. Unfortunately he was prevented from saying goodbye in person. But his father would not send juvenile-correction officers on his trail or order him back with threatening missives. His father was a good and clever man. From now on he would go his own way, filling up his days in melancholy content. Marie Thérèse was still at his side, and she was his child.

But he still wanted to say goodbye to her, he wanted to wake her up at all costs and tell her that he had to go on a journey.

He ran back up to her room, and it struck him that just last night he had been to "take leave" of her. But this time he did not move so cautiously. This farewell was of a louder, morning-light variety. The little child was still sleeping in her tiny bed, but the bigger child was already setting out on his exploits:—that was the way of it.

He tugged at her nightgown and tickled her under the chin. Then she woke right up. "Is it morning already?" she said and smiled right in his face, although she was still so drunk with sleep she had to blink her eyes. And, with a brighter voice than she had ever heard him use, he said, "Don't you see? The sky is already quite blue—," and they both laughed up at the sky that shimmered between the trees in the garden in its bluish gray and morning chill.

Then, embarrassed, leaning over the bed, he told her hastily, "I have to go on a trip just now—yes, imagine that, right at the peep of dawn—for a long time—rather long at the start—I really don't know how long it'll be."—She had sat up in her tiny bed, kneeling in her little nightgown between the pillows. "Oh," she said in jest and turned her silk-smooth, transformed little face tilting up to his, "is little Andreas going away? Then I have to cry"—and she let her head almost drop into her creased little hand and crouched in a let's-pretend posture of grief in her bed, as fond and teasing as the blessed angels are. "Say goodbye to Peterchen for me," her brother said and put his mouth to her small warm hands, "don't forget"—and he was gone.

Marie Thérèse pretended for a few more moments, cunning and lost in thought, until she lay back in sleep.—

As soon as Andreas was standing down in the garden, he ran back up the steps once more to his workroom on the second story. He had forgot something.

Quite out of breath, he hurried upstairs. In every corner, rushed, panting, distraught, he looked for something. At last he found it: a large gray cloth, an old canvas rag. And he threw the rag over his picture, threw it over the incomplete depiction of the Good Lord, Who stood in the morning light cold and melancholy. Now it was veiled, like a dead man beneath a graceful shroud.

* * *

Ursula Bischof also found a letter on the breakfast table first thing, which Andreas had left for her early in the morning. The servant said, "The young gentleman dropped off the letter himself. I saw it out the kitchen window. He looked a bit excited—"

Ursula hesitated a moment before opening it. Her eyes displayed profound anxiety, her hands trembled too. But she read it nevertheless.

When she came to the end she did not immediately raise her head. She kept it quietly bowed over the paper. Not until her father came in did she look up. She said "Good morning" and passed him the tea. But he shot a rapid glance at her and realized that her eyes were filled with tears. He had never seen his daughter cry before.

When she turned back to her letter and read it over again, she was able to smile. And her father recognized the smile as well, although it sat so hard and impenetrable on her face.

They sat across from one another, the father who had already experienced everything in his loneliness, and the daughter, near to him, and yet waiting for the one who in arrogance, pride and sorrow had set off to experience the essentials, in his own way.

And so the girl's gaze strayed from her father's face which confronted her with wise, yet uninquisitive eyes, down to her little letter, written so gruffly, so disgracefully abruptly, so haughtily, and which she would have liked to put to her lips.

And so her hard smile blessed the letter and he who had written it. This smile shed a blessing on him, a blessing on his earnest game, a blessing on the pious dance.

Two

1

WHEN he arrived in Berlin, evening was drawing on and it was rather dark. There was no point in calling for a porter and handing over his suitcase—he discovered there were far too few porters provided considering the number of travelers, there was even a terrible hue and cry after these individuals—and so, on his own, he lugged the heavy bag to a car. Pulled downstairs sideways by the burden, he staggered across the platform. His entrance into the city was somewhat lopsided.

Andreas timidly put the question to a cab driver who sat, stern and mustachioed in his leather jacket, whether he might know of a room for him—a furnished room—nothing too expensive, but not too shabby either. The man with the mustache surveyed him from head to foot in some surprise. Andreas had to shut his eyes before this inexorable scrutiny. So this is how people would look at him. And he offered his face to this man, the first man in this ruthless city. His face was gray and drawn from the journey, his eyes hot and strained. A tremor quivered around his mouth as if he were about to cry.

The scrutiny apparently had not been unfavorable. "Awright," said the driver, "get in then—rooms is pretty hard to find these days.—But I think my wife has got one left to give, rent, I mean."—And Andreas got in, bent beneath the weight of his suitcase, for the man in the leather jacket, though relatively obliging, could conceive of nothing in the world stranger than helping this somewhat suspect adolescent in the long yellow overcoat with the disheveled hair and strained eyes with his burden. And now Andreas was sitting in the jolting vehicle—all alone with his suitcase.

His thoughts were painfully focused on money matters and could not be drawn, even momentarily, from urgent and extremely distressing topics. All he kept thinking was: All right—now I'll get a room—but how much will it cost? I can certainly take it for a week with the money I have left. And then I'll have to earn some more. But how—how will I earn it?—Well, that's the reason I made my move, after all, to find that out.—Yes, then I'll have to earn some more.—

His head, which offered no resistance to the movement of the vehicle, kept shaking up and down. He rode through this strange city, his head wobbling, with only a single weary, harsh, crippling thought: "Yes, then I'll have to earn some—earn some—"

All along the way the city shone with arc lamps and flashing electric signs. The city did not care about him sitting alone in the vehicle. Every so often, though, it shot a small, dazzling sidelight on him through the window—an arc lamp would flicker on his face, drooping in weariness, as if it wanted to test his mettle in passing, as the cabman had tested him before.

They drove for a long time, hours long it seemed to Andreas. They stopped for the first time when the streets had become narrower and darker. "All right," the cabman said hoarsely as he opened the car door, "there'll be a room for you here—I can recommend it."—And he actually laughed.

The stairwell smelled unappetizing. Half honey and half rotten eggs.—Andreas was barely able to breathe. But escape was, of course, impossible. The broad-backed cabman was trudging on, only one step ahead of him.

The cabman's wife, gray-haired and raw-boned, walked sulkily out of her kitchen. Yes, she opined, her arms folded in front of her, the room is still available. She had suddenly put on a pair of glasses and was obliquely, maliciously scrutinizing this peculiar youngster standing so pale by his little suitcase. "But you've got to pay in advance," she said and mercilessly shook her head as she fussily removed her glasses from her nose, "ten marks minimum."—And Andreas, who had not even seen the room yet, blushed and fumbled in his wallet.

Meanwhile the cabman himself had opened the door and stood broad-shouldered in the doorway. Andreas thought him to be more prepossessing than his mate, despite the reek of sweat and tobacco that struck him forcefully as the man strode ahead of him into the room. Yes, it could certainly not be called luxurious. He would probably take down the big picture of majestic ex-Kaiser Wilhelm if he stayed here any longer, and hang something of his own up there. The washstand would certainly remain spindly and dirty, the linoleum greasy.

But as the landlady headed back to her kitchen, she asked him whether perhaps she might not send in her daughter, to help him with his unpacking. Before he could reply, the daughter was there. Andreas blushed again and said he expected he could manage by himself. She was wearing a green silk blouse, thrusting out her bosom before her like a precious treasure, and laughed at him, winking her bright blue pop-eyes. "Ah," she said, and he was alarmed for her voice was even more nasal than he had expected, "we can do it together." And she stepped with alluring stride a few paces closer to him. "Or maybe you'd like to go out again? Want a little escape, lots of excitement—right?" She chaffed him and gaily waved her plump manicured hands. "But we don't really have to do that—"

Suddenly she sat down and began to explain that she worked as a hairdresser by day.—"Yes," she reported earnestly, "my employers are very comfortably set up"—but she was free nights, her own mistress.—

Andreas, standing in front of the black windows, had closed his eyes as a wave of nausea washed over him. But suddenly he turned away with a surprisingly forceful, indeed harsh movement, and looked at the street. "Good night," he said and his voice had taken on a different tone.

The timbre of his voice caused the girl to withdraw. She tidied her reddish hair with a few petulant gestures. She pursed her lips and said a few times, "Thanks ever so—thanks ever so," and, fat and haughty, went out the door.

"I happen to be tired," Andreas said quietly behind her, "excuse me, I simply want to get some sleep."—But she uttered a last, resolute "Thanks ever so," and slammed the door behind her.

The youth at the window turned his face to the street again. He opened the window a bit and held out his face to the cool darkness. The lamps swayed in a long row. But the houses across the way were quite dark. Many strange dark houses. Andreas looked at them and froze a bit at the sight. All full of life, all full of secrets.—

Suddenly a dog darted somewhere or other, and there were sounds of awful howling and derisive laughter. It terrified him. He stepped back into the room, intimidated. Pensively he walked back and forth.—Perhaps he had been a little too hostile to the young lady, he wondered anxiously. She certainly had no fiendish intentions. He was just some "young gentleman" to her.—And it was quite right to try and take advantage of the situation. But why was her bosom so unpleasantly rigid beneath the cheap silk?

He could hear her outside, already insulting him. "That one's still wet behind the ears," she said shrilly and her parents muttered responses from another region. She seemed, by the way, still eager to go out. Furiously she demanded her coat and her best hat.

Andreas had to smile at that. It tickled him that she chose her best hat. As if the most ordinary one would not have done as well. And how seductively she would wear this bit of finery beneath the swaying lamps.

He decided he did not want to unpack today. The best thing would be to go right to sleep. That way his room too would be dark and not attract the attention of the black row of houses. Any reflective passerby would think, there's someone asleep in there.—And yet he was that someone, Andreas Magnus, the individual, he who sallied forth knowing not whither,—only because he had solemnly vowed he would at a time which, even now, had retreated into the past as impenetrably as a fairy tale.

He had to smile again at what he was—a ludicrous adventurer in the sight of God—just as he had smiled at the best hat of the girl who liked outings. Smiling he undressed and smiling he got in bed.

Although the pillows felt greasy and smelled, faintly but thoroughly, of all sorts of imponderables, he lay on them nevertheless, full of confidence.

He fell asleep almost as soon as he turned out the light.

His head had slipped sideways off the pillows. His hands lay clasped beside his face.

2

His sleep was troubled, something he had never known before. He had waked frequently, felt hot and uncomfortable, and his couch nauseated him.

He also woke much earlier in the morning than he was used to, the day still looked gray outside the windows. But all at once, as soon as he awoke, he realized clearly what the dull sense of malaise was that had tormented him all night long. He needed only to look at his hands, red and swollen as they were. He needed only to look at his body: all along his back, down his legs to his burning feet: the individual bites could barely be distinguished from the mass. Everything was red, hard, irritated, swollen.

He sprang out of bed, but his feet were repelled by the greasy linoleum. He ran to the mirror, which was opaque and speckled. Such a stifling, even overwhelming feeling of having been victimized, profoundly humiliated and disgraced came over him that, with his face pressed against the cool mirror, he had to weep—in bitter indignation, all alone, twitching and naked in his room. He had bites even behind his ears and all over his neck and a great portion of his forehead, shoving up his right eye in sympathetic ugliness.

Still weeping he got dressed. A savage desire came over him to tear down the ex-Kaiser's portrait and smash it on the bed. But he would not waste the energy.

He immediately put on his overcoat, for under no circumstances would he breakfast there. Then he rang.

The cab driver's wife showed up, unprepossessing in her apron, her arms folded before her as if she had never been to bed. With a sullen sidelong look, she measured the swollen face of her guest, who sat on the bed in an overcoat, smoking cigarettes in his despair.

"Naturally, I shall have to move," Andreas said calmly, his voice trembling a bit. "You can see for yourself, I've been bitten all over." And suddenly a little more loudly, something in his face quivering as if he would break into tears again: "There are bugs in this bed—"

The cabman's wife scarcely listened. She was already on

her sullen way out. "Yes," was all she said—and her arms remained stuck to her body—"if the gentleman doesn't like it here—"

After she had left the room, Andreas sat motionless on the bed a few more minutes—motionless in an overcoat on the strange bed that had disgraced him. Now he had to look for another room—he had forfeited ten marks into the bargain—

He stood up awkwardly, grasped the suitcase and slowly withdrew from the room.

He was not prepared for what awaited him outside. At the kitchen door, father, mother and daughter stood like a trio, as if drawn up for some threatening military review—the stocky cabman in shirt-sleeves, his mate with the twinkling glasses on her nose, the daughter, buxom and flushed in a flame-colored satin dressing gown.—Barely had Andreas left his room and was standing across from them in isolation when their passionately unanimous insults commenced.

"Never," raved the father's bass voice, "never in all my life have I heard of such a thing! Bedbugs, he says—Bedbugs—" And meanwhile the mother was scolding from her central position: "Bugs in my house! In my house bugs! Who knows where he's been hanging around nights!" And the daughter in the thick of it, her dyed hair in disarray, her fat red face powdered in haste: "And him so young, just think of it! Just think of it, him so young!"—as if this were the supreme reproach that put all the others in the shade. The whole family seemed to take up this theme in every vocal pitch, bellowing to raise the roof: "Such impudence—just think of it, him so young! Bedbugs! And so young at that!!!"

Andreas fumbled past them to the door. He would have liked to turn around and say something too, perhaps a kind of explanation. But the cabman, taking a couple of menacing steps in his direction, loomed over him frighteningly. "We don't want any discussions with you," he blurted as he raised his arms, "you're too young for us! Clear out, before you get a good bash on the ear to send you packing! The impudence!"

Stupefied, Andreas staggered down the stairs. Behind him that accusation, the bitter, impassioned insult that he was, of all things, young—very young, of all things—resounded maliciously behind him.

The street outside was gray and uninviting. It was so long and straight that its end was out of sight. Just a suburban street, of course, but probably one of the most important, a major suburban thoroughfare.

A man came whistling down the street, Andreas could see him in the distance. He was holding something in his hand that moved slightly, and at the last moment Andreas recognized what it was. The whistler was carrying a chicken by its neck; it dangled as casually pendulous as if it were a wrapped package, although it was living and jerking.—The sight made Andreas put down his suitcase, as if a short, sickeningly well-aimed jab had been made at his nerves.

He stood in the long suburban street and thought, as the flood of tears welled up in him again and his mouth quivered: Why is the world so ugly? I sallied forth, full of confidence in it, even though another path, a more noiseless path by far attracted me. And at the very outset it shows itself in such unmitigated hideousness that I must regret I didn't keep away from it.

Then he thought he had better visit a barber, for he was unshaven too. A sign for one was hanging behind him. He hoped he hadn't chosen the man with the jerking hen.

The barber's was not a particularly pleasant experience either. The man who waited on him turned out to be small, indeed, almost stunted. He had the hard, cold hands of an orang-utan and, in addition, wore eyeglasses for an operation which involved such great responsibility, and there was something suspicious about his nearsightedness too. The other assistant—the one with red, close-cropped hair and unblinking eyes, who, incidentally, made an even more unnerving impression—addressed him as "Professor"—for no clear reason.

Andreas, his face covered with lather, sat in the chair and looked woeful. When the "Professor" operated with his razor and his bizarre myopia, and tried pawkily to tease him about his bug bites, all he got in reply was a dismal smile. Everything hurt so badly, the bites behind his ears were the keenest, they burned like an abscess. And when, almost by accident, he caught sight of his face in the mirror, he felt like sinking through the floor in a surfeit of shame, on account of his absurdly swollen eyes.

On the other hand, there was nothing in his immediate environment to tempt him to regard it closely or lovingly. Directly before him on the marble tabletop was a small bowl filled with an almost blood-red fluid, in which a little yellowish object floated. It actually looked like an artfully amputated human organ, something along the lines of a heart or a spleen, that had been put aside in its own blood.—Andreas closed his eyes again.—So that's what this world is like. Did this little thing have to go on jerking too, as the chicken had before?—It was but cold comfort and superficial consolation to tell himself that it was only a little yellow sponge, floating in a liquid that had been tinted red to look pretty.

How early it was still when he was finally able to leave the small painful barbershop and the endless gray street lay before him once more. At least it was an expanse, although a depressing one, an expanse after that cluttered, vilely perfumed constriction.

Now he wanted breakfast, yes, he was hungry too. Close at hand he found a sort of tavern that served food. Things were certainly convenient around here.

He could barely look at the waiters. They were sleepy and

wore such greasy jackets. They merely scrutinized him as a person who had just walked in.—He ordered something from someone. Then he sat at his wooden table with his face in his hands. He felt as if his face were sorely wounded.

All he felt was a slight, rather faint, almost melancholy doubt as to whether he could bring it off. It was such hard going. And besides, he had virtually no purpose.—Of course, he never once suggested going back home. His pride found it preferable by far to be an incompetent on this toilsome path and broken by its cruelty than to return to the home that would take him in again with desperately excruciating and yet arrogant effort; the home whose hopelessness he had wanted to escape by that pathway to silence and then, afterwards, by this other, arduous, adventurous way out. But why did the adventure have to be so unpleasant—

He had finally stopped packing his heart with complaints that everything had to be this way, so ugly and merciless, or with charges against others for having arranged things in this incomprehensible manner. All he felt was surprise, a great and bitter surprise. This feeling of surprise made him so ill that he felt he had to lay his weary head on the table.—But there was another customer sitting in the background of the tavern who actually seemed to be observing him, so he drew himself up and sat very still, lest he divulge something.

As it happened, this customer strode boldly across the whole room and came up to him. She was a lady wearing a small dark red trilby tipped over her forehead and a big white fur twisted round her neck that buried her chin. She had very black eyes, which would squint as if near-sighted. She spoke to Andreas in a gruff voice and a somewhat foreign accent. "You haven't been in Berlin very long?" she said and sized him up with a gloomily thorough glance.

*

The lady's name was Fräulein Franziska and she turned out to be well disposed towards him. "I can spot a stranger in this city right away," she said and laughed darkly, "you all have a funny look in your eyes—" and she linked the strangers with funny looks in their eyes to this mysterious "you." She was not a native either, but was Russian by birth, brought up in Paris and married somewhere else again. That was all she said about herself. But she wanted to know about him, his occupation, his trade. Since he was evasive and provided vague information, she suddenly said—without the glimmer of a smile, but with a good deal of pragmatism in her rough voice: "You got any money?"—whereupon he lowered his eyes as if he were standing before a suddenly insurmountable obstacle. Still, he did answer—in a trembling voice: "Yes—for a while—" and then sat very still and simply let her pursue the subject. Up to now the question had never presented itself to him in such a stark and direct manner. With downcast eyes and a heart full of fear, he realized that all the danger and dirtiness of this desperate life was compressed into this question, like some monstrous and colossal symbol. Then he felt that convulsion, that nausea of loathing that had shaken him when he was **alone before the mirror in the cabman's wife's room pulse** through his body again.—Fräulein Franziska also wanted information about the bug bites.

They soon came to an agreement. It appeared that he was in want of a roof, so the lady, never diverting her deep, searching, concentrated gaze from his face that was an open book to her, recommended that he follow her at once to Meyerstein's Boarding House, where a room had just become available—little Petra had had to leave, she'd run out of money—and where he would find stimulating companionship. "I live there too," the lady said and emitted her curt, deep, impassive and yet mysterious laugh.

She may be a criminal, Andreas reflected, somewhat

edified by his previous experiences. Her skin was remarkably dirty, very raw and ravaged. She was made-up heavily but recklessly, almost chaotically: her mouth was smeared brick-red and some of the paint had even got on her teeth: one eyetooth was as red as if dipped in blood, which gave her a dangerous look.—Intending a subtle test to get wind of her motives, Andreas asked her—and felt himself an initiate into all the world's wiles—"What's in it for you, I wonder, once you've lured me to this boarding house I know nothing about? Would you please let me know it now?"—But she did not avert her eyes from his face, which made him feel all the warmer—he could feel them on his forehead. "A kid!" was all she said. Then he saw that though her face was stern, it was good-natured and kindly.

So he rose and went with her.—

Meyerstein's Boarding House was located on the third floor of a not unappealing, bright gray tenement. The street teemed with trams and buses, but lay in a better neighborhood and had a certain elegance.

Frau Meyerstein, with a roast-beef face and a white blouse, invited the new tenant into her own sitting room. "An old friend of mine," Fräulein Franziska explained vaguely and stood to one side in her fur and her little trilby. Widow Meyerstein spoke a rather obscure dialect, Andreas noticed at once. She had been born in Würzburg and the Swabian element was predominant. But her late husband had been an English engineer and she had spent years in London with him. Swabian and English—two difficult dialects at best—combined in her to form an impossible hybrid. "You're cordially welcome," she said and her red face laughed constantly.— Suddenly she introduced her mother, who had been sitting somewhere unnoticed the whole time. Her large staring head nodded across the sewing table; she had white, severely kempt hair and apoplectic blue cheeks. Frau Meyerstein's little daughter too was suddenly on hand, creeping out from behind her skirts, as if she were kept within their folds. Her name was Henriette and she had a small white big-city child's face, the mouth too red and the eyes inflamed. Her sharp, gray gaze measured Andreas. "My little filly," said the widow and her fleshy face and flashing eyes laughed barbarically.

The three of them—the staring grandmother, the laughing mother, the cunning child—had something fear-inspiring about them, to be sure—but something touching as well.

Later he was left alone with Fräulein Franziska in his new room. It was surprisingly large and must at one time have been a dining room or a reception room. It was probably noisy, Andreas noted, for the three large windows opened on to the street.

Fräulein Franziska, suddenly tired, sat heavily on the bed, a cigarette in her mouth. Andreas remarked for the first time that she was dressed in a very slovenly fashion, her skirt and stockings hung down oddly. But the color combination and the quality of the material were both good. Incidentally she reminded him of someone, but he could not say who.

"How much money do you actually have right now?" she suddenly asked and directed her gaze at him again. And, standing at the door in his overcoat, he quietly confessed, "I've got eighty-five marks left." She did not take her eyes off him but merely said, "We'll find something for you. After your bug bites go away.—Sit by me on the bed." And Andreas walked across the big room and sat beside her.

"Henriette is no good," she said after a long pause and shook her head earnestly, "a wicked child."—But Andreas smiled at that. "Ah," he said, "children are never bad if you treat them right." And he seemed to see Marie Thérèse and her tiny cavalier standing before him. "Yes," he heard the stranger at his side say as if from a distance, "that's true all right."

In the course of the day he became acquainted with the rest

of the boarders, who were exclusively young people. In a short, impartial summing-up, Fräulein Franziska told him the essentials about each one.

There was Fräulein Barbara, fat and mannish in her blue suit, with her big childish face comically topped by a kind of tall silk hat. "Glad to meet you, my boy!" she said and joyfully held out her broad hand in its brown leather glove.—She had made a clean break with her short, rich, Jewish stepfather, Fräulein Franziska reported curtly, although he had maintained her comfortably, indeed luxuriously in his mansion in Nuremberg. Full of ingratitude, she had flown the coop and her father could not find out where she was staying. What she worked at every day was something Fräulein Franziska could hardly say. Most likely she went in for shady speculations and trafficked with young gentlemen from the Stock Exchange, but perhaps she simply worked in a dress shop. In addition, although she carried on an ostentatious liaison with a pallid ballerina who often spent the night with her, she kept up a certain gushing fondness for Paulchen, the dancer who was Franziska's colleague.—Colleague?—Andreas did not know what she meant. But his friend calmly replied, "Yes, we work together in a cabaret and we're often together afterwards as well."

Nor was Paulchen slow in putting in an appearance. He minced out of his brightly furnished little room, his shoulders hunched nervously, in a bright yellow quilted housecoat with a red carnation in its buttonhole. Hurriedly and somewhat obliquely he bowed to Fräulein Franziska's new friend and the hand he offered him was cool and light. "Very nice," he said in a high squeaking voice and pursed his carefully made-up lady's lips anxiously. His face, neatly treated with all sorts of colognes and essences, was as white as milk and emptier than any face Andreas had ever seen. The eyes in this face that looked out at Andreas were lackluster and heart-rendingly dull. "The three of us should be nice and cozy together," said Paulchen and shrugged his shoulders.

Fräulein Lisa, the professional artist, also introduced herself. Slim and blonde, with rather hard blazing eyes, she smiled at Andreas. She kept her hands in the deep pockets of her green wool jacket and moved like one of those silly women who play a lot of sports—affected and tomboyish at the same time. She certainly gave no impression that she was avidly involved in the lofty doctrines of the theosophical and anthroposophist schools. By day she made dancing blackamoors out of wool and painted little lopsided bottles.

Everyone took supper together in Frau Meyerstein's room. The table was a bit small for so many persons and the seating was cramped. But Frau Meyerstein, laughing barbarically, presided at the upper end of the table. She too had a guest, a Professor Sonn, who sat beside her. The gentleman was an instructor at the technical high school, but lively and congenial, with thick hair, a checked suit and a white mustache. The rumor ran that he was making a play for Frau Meyerstein's widowed hand, a rumor that struck no one as incredible. But for all his genteel joviality, he had unpleasant, treacherous eyes that harbored no good intentions.

Fräulein Anna, who spent her days mutely and diligently in her room with bast, linen and metal, also put in an appearance. She came in fat and short in a coarse linen smock, but her broad Buddha face, which somehow always looked begrimed even when freshly washed, was the most placid of them all.

The lamp illuminated their faces as brightly as if it meant to expose them utterly and strip away the mask from each one. Down the length of the table the Professor, who was well-traveled, was saying, "Yes, yes—London has to be explored, you have to stay in London for a month—Paris is all on display."—And Frau Meyerstein laughed till her eyes disappeared entirely in her roast-beef face and she had to cough.

But none of the young people was looking up at her. At the lower end Fräulein Barbara was speaking loudly and boldly about trotting races and was also appraising the prospects of a certain boxer. "It's awfully thrilling," she said and there was excitement in her big, heavily powdered child's face, "but I still think—"

Meanwhile Paulchen was telling Franziska's new friend, Andreas, to whose face he glued his lackluster eyes, racy bits of gossip, which he laughed at himself with a squeal. "I'm tellin' ya," he would cry whenever there was an especially mysterious punchline, and then he would always underline it with an assertion: "That Doctor Dorfbaum—no! That Doctor Dorfbaum!"

With blazing eyes Fräulein Lisa was telling industrious Fräulein Anna about the esoteric doctrines that consumed her with interest. "What would man be otherwise?" she said and smiled deliriously. But Fräulein Anna, grimy and stout, was the most silent of them all. "They can't come up with an answer to that," said Fräulein Lisa preachily, "but think of it: the ladder to purification—." Fräulein Barbara put her arm around Lisa's shoulder. "Lisa kid," she said and laughed winningly at her like a young man, "that trotting race yesterday—But you got so carried away with Dempsey—." And Fräulein Lisa, suddenly interested just as ardently in this matter, replied, resigning herself to the embracing pressure of Barbara's arm, "How could I know, precious—everything was against it—"

Whereupon Paulchen lay his light hand on Fräulein Franziska's heavy one which was busy with knife and fork. "Sister," he drawled, "I'm telling ya—and I was just letting our Andreas know it too: that Doctor Dorfbaum—honestly!" And his eyes and eyebrows shot up with shock.

But suddenly Widow Meyerstein leaned forward a bit in

her chair and said so loudly above the talk that the speakers fell dumb, "Fräulein Barbara, I forgot this morning to call your attention to the fact that if you don't pay me forty marks tomorrow morning, one, you'll have to leave my boarding house, and, two, I'll write to your respected father in Nuremberg for the money I'm owed."

In a flash everyone had become very serious. All the faces, mouths tightly shut, eyes filled with fear, were turned to the widow, enthroned in her white blouse, unctuous in her majesty. With a certain severe courtesy she now addressed Andreas—so confident was she, so conscious of her power once the conversation settled on this particular subject: "Around here it's pay by the week, dear Herr Magnus, as she knows well enough. Fräulein Barbara has not yet cleared up all of last week's debt, and this one not at all. I cannot put up with it." And she shook her head deliberately, while she drummed her fingers on the table.—Andreas looked at her and read in her eyes the anguish he had noticed before in the others. The great symbol stood before him, the great potentate, the ugly, merciless majesty in whose brutal, authoritarian face all things were compacted, and what it meant to be subject to material wants. "I cannot put up with it," said her roast-beef face. And Andreas felt the doubt as never before: would he be able to endure it? It promised to be hard—

Behind the lenses of his pince-nez Professor Sonn observed the scene with unsympathetic eyes. In the end one could always manage these children, who never got good marks for their bad conduct.—Glassy-eyed and alert, the apoplectic grandmother blinked around the room.—Henriette sat almost pinched and shriveled in her bright blue ribbons and let the others talk.—The widow went on drumming.

But Andreas looked at the young people, his contemporaries, one after the other. And he saw how small, almost imperceptible wrinkles circled their mouths, and realized that early adventures, precocious misery, immature suffering had carved them there. It struck him that all of them, essentially alien to the world, essentially just children more than any other young people had ever been, had been waging a premature battle which their ambition and their need forced them to endure, although it was far too harsh for them. They compressed their lips: the symbol of the battle, the hated, feared, beloved symbol stood before them—the talk was of money. Their eyes were closed too. But Andreas's passion for intellectual curiosity tried to read something into those eyes that would betray nothing. Perhaps he hoped to learn from them a kind of secret or talisman, that then would help him too, would keep him from going under in the battle. He saw himself in all of them.

Fräulein Lisa, so sporty and yet so full of occult learning, kept her blazing eyes coyly downcast. But Andreas knew that the narrow and peculiar dogma that burned in them could not be the mystery he sought. Fräulein Barbara, still imposing but now mostly depressed, which was only natural, gnawed her lip like a scolded child who had turned moody—and yet that mouth was so carelessly painted.—Fräulein Franziska, good-humored and objective, squinted and peered.—Paulchen, pale as milk and nervous, anxiously sniffed at his light, perfumed hands.

But then their talk spilled forth once more. Suddenly they were talking about remote, gross things, bloody events in China were described. One fat minister had had his belly slit and filled with live rats.—His shrill ministerial screams could be heard throughout the entire countryside. The gnawing beasts were making their way out from the inside.—Barbara injected the name Karl May into the discussion and oratorically praised him to the skies. "This is the truth," she repeated. "Children! this is the beginning!"

Andreas thought of the words, desperate and proud, which

he had once heard. "But," a girl had said, "what is our youth all about? Our younger generation has no ardor at all," he heard her voice, "like a coward it disavows its sorrow and will not learn from it. Ah, it thinks it has such a simple way out of the confusion—" But she believed in her father, who was a hero, because in loneliness he had endured what was essential and created works of art from it.

Now he sat, a helpless, thoughtful adventurer, among those the voice had scorned—he sat amongst them and brooded. Perhaps they would never create works of art. Perhaps that is not the way it ought to be. At home his torment and effort stood draped with a sheet like a dead man. Perhaps the children who were there were a new power, already capable of making progress. For after all these tormenting thoughts, he soon suspected that he, Andreas, and this generation would launch something new on earth.

The "grown-ups" spoke about literature from the upper end of the table. Frau Meyerstein declared that she was mad about Dickens, but Professor Sonn revealed to her that Dickens was out of date. "Nevertheless," the widow asserted, "books are my favorite dish," at which she laughed until she coughed convulsively. Professor Sonn laughed with her as did the rachitic Henriette, whose pinched and bitter laughter had an uncanny effect, as if someone were hurting her.—But beneath the laughter Andreas could hear Fräulein Lisa's lightly cooing voice, "The Christ was a unique event, whereas this victory—"

Whereupon they arose from the table.

After the meal Fräulein Franziska and Paulchen had to go to the cabaret where they worked. Andreas escorted them but was tired and saw very little.

He sat in a small red box, which they had shown him to, his eyes half closed and a cigarette between his fingers. While his friends changed clothes, he watched the preceding act. It was

Alma Zeiserich, the board of directors and management of the whole affair. Skinny and spiteful she stood in a gold brocade gown and sang her indecent songs in an ice-cold manner, flinging her facial expressions at the house. One of the songs concerned a trip to the potty, which provided much opportunity for puns. "Well, well, anyway," went the refrain that Frau Zeiserich used to wind up her amusing verses, "that's the big job—so folks say"—and her voice was as cold as sheet metal.

Andreas preferred to close his eyes until Franziska came on stage. But even then he barely saw, as through a veil, a sort of apache girl before the curtain, amid the noise, a red scarf about her neck. Her voice came to him as through a veil as well, her raw, hard, leaden voice. "And since that day I've loved them all," she sang and her voice sailed gaily, impartially and sharply over the red rag, "the prime of life is what I have. And when my charms from off me fall, I'll gladly sink into my grave—" Uncomplaining, full of unembittered, hard-won knowledge the girl's voice called these words to him. Her enunciation made it clear to him for the first time how inaccurate her German was. But then she was a Russian and brought up in Paris.—And then the crowd took up her drawn-out, vibrant, thrilling tune.

Then she squinted her eyes, which for the first time had grown big, black and staring, and pursed her lips, and with a slightly grimacing but otherwise frozen face, she spun out a long ballad, a litany of symmetrical verses of comical and gruesome subject matter. It was full of grotesque pain, a lame dog, an old poet and a virgin. And one could almost see Fräulein Franziska sprouting a beard—a black, untamed murderer's beard—around her painted face, when her coarse voice recounted unflinchingly:

A maid of forty, it's a fact,
Had kept her maidenhead intact,
Her maidenhead intact.

She must be punished well, God sneered,
And made her sprout a bushy beard,
She sprouts a bushy beard.

And, even half asleep, Andreas could not help but observe a great crop of bushy whiskers hanging on this remarkable damsel's face.—Then she shook them off, sang the severe and derisive moral of the song, bowed in bitter earnest and walked off in her ridiculous cabaret costume.

Following her, Paulchen danced. A sweet, sentimental magical little tune wafted up from the orchestra, and Paulchen, up to his chin in violet silk, flew weightlessly, wingèd, thoughtless as a drooping leaf, yielding the curves, the fanciful bends of his body between the curtains and before the footlights; he slid to the ground, as if expiring, rose up again, straightened out, expanded, enraptured, carried along by the motion with which he raised his arms, outstretched them, extended himself to the utmost on tiptoe, balancing, trembling, vibrating, as if he wanted to fly off into space, ascending unhampered into the night—his head bent somewhat to one side, his empty, light head, the mouth half-opened, the black painted eyes dimmed as though intoxicated.—This dance was called "A Bird's Evening Prayer." He had thought up the title himself.

He bowed, suddenly frail and bleached in the light, and in a flash Andreas, his face propped up, felt seized by a deep compassion, which he himself did not understand, as the opaque, lackluster gaze reached out of this milk-white, brainless, rigid face, met his and grazed it.—

Franziska and Paulchen came into his box later, said they had to go out again, and would he like to join them. But he was too tired and thanked them. Incidentally he now saw for the first time the severity and oddity of Franziska's ornaments. She wore an imperial cape of white ermine and a high heron's feather nodded above her face. A great many bracelets jangled on her arm, too.—Behind her Paulchen stood anxiously, wearing a pleated lady's cape and a big light-gray fedora.—On his way out, Andreas also noticed for the first time that the cabaret where Franziska sang was flatly called "The Mudhole." This had not previously attracted his attention.

In his big room he fell asleep as quickly as he had the night before—and in a moment, as if he had taken a sleeping powder. Naturally, he had at first been worried by this new bed, for he was still unacquainted with its dangers. But this night too his hands were clasped as he fell asleep.

***

Late at night he woke up again—or was it getting on for morning?—A face was leaning over his bed. It was mottled and severe and yet full of soothing warmth. He could not recognize it. He only felt it speak a few words towards him, saying: "Asleep already? Then sleep well, my little Andreas—," and it kept bending closer to him, perhaps to his mouth. It was as kind as the face of a mother, gentle as that of a lover after the first night, mysterious as the face of a sister. It was as full of contradictions as the face of life itself. The sleeper stared at it, failed to understand it, but lay there with clasped hands like one who has faith that some day everything will come clear.

Meanwhile, next door, Widow Meyerstein was still awake, alone, after everyone had gone. The light in her eyes, which otherwise gleamed so merrily and cruelly, seemed extinguished. It was as if bright blue glass eyes had been implanted in her broad womanly face. Her mother, still staring and haggard, sat beside her. "Fräulein Barbara had better pay up," said the widow. But she received no answer. Her mother, whom she wanted to talk with, only stared attentively and in bewilderment around the room with her blue face. Then her daughter suddenly raised both hands, as in an abrupt gesture of terror. But it was only to fix her hairdo. Her red, yet sedulously manicured fingers dug hard into her hair.—

Outside in the pitch-dark corridor Fräulein Barbara and Fräulein Franziska ran into one another. Fräulein Franziska said—for no particular reason, and her voice was fainter than usual—, "Andreas is asleep already."—And Fräulein Barbara hastily asked in reply, "Is Paulchen home yet?" To which Fräulein Franziska responded, "No—he's with friends—" At that the fat girl only drooped her face. As if she had suddenly become paralyzed, her heavy body moved away. She had been frantic the whole night, collecting money.—

In her room Frau Meyerstein leaned over the ice cold cot in which her child, pinched and hostile, was slumbering. "How charming she looks," she said with a laborious, wooden compassion and turned back to her mother. But the old woman only stared and sat silent.

No real communication could take place between the two women.

4

In the morning Henriette waked him. Of course she did not touch him, but rather stood mute at the foot of the bed with his breakfast. Yet beneath her keen gray gaze he stirred, turned his face amid the pillows, sighed, tried to smile,—but the smile fled from his face once more—and opened his eyes. He looked at Henriette, quickly scrutinized her small, white, sickly face, her closed, pinched countenance with the excessively red protruding mouth, the bulging forehead, the hair plastered down with water—but then his glance slipped from her and slid wearily into the strange, big boarding house room. Every morning he felt all over again as if he were waking up in a hotel room where for the first time he had had to spend a single, stifling, dreamless night and which looked foreign to him when he awoke—utterly foreign with the cheap carpet, the washstand and the little bookcase. From his narrow, white bed which stood pressed against the wall, shabbily titivated with a lace tester, he looked round, not exactly in annoyance, but distressed by the state of things. His breakfast lay before him on a round tray, half sunk into the feather bed. But he ignored it, for he had long been aware that they did not know how to brew tea. He had been living here for a week now. Where had the days gone?—He didn't know any more, he didn't want to remember. The one sweet longing that invaded him was to close his eyes again. To shut out the carpet and Henriette and the washstand and look upon the darkness that waited for him within.

But Henriette's voice, small and coarse like a cheap musical instrument, terrorized him. "Frau Meyerstein requires a settlement from you today," she said, standing before him thin in a little washdress, as she spoke of her mother the way a dwarfish maid-of-all-work might speak of the mistress she devoutly fears, "the widow definitely doesn't like to be kept waiting."—And quietly she made her exit.

Later Andreas dropped in on Fräulein Franziska, who was sitting calmly before a little marble table eating an ample breakfast. Each time he came in he was horrified anew by the disorderliness of her room. Stockings, skirts, liquor bottles, newspapers lay in heaps on top of each other. The white fur hung over a stand like a bathtowel. As a rickety ornament, a tambourine dangled, red and Hispanic, from the wall. Castanets hung beside it. As a matter of fact, Fräulein Franziska had spent a year in Madrid and was actually a subject of the Spanish empire.

She had tidied up this morning. She cut herself big pink slices of ham, and when Andreas, nervously toying with a cigarette, remarked that his money was gone and he could barely meet the week's rent and said "Now what?," she merely replied, "Pooh, pooh" and ate more breakfast. Then she began to explain. She had seen it coming, oh yes, the eighty-five marks, the slender bankroll, the precious cash—it was all used up. But she had already come up with an idea. She laughed mysteriously at him, her lap covered with a big napkin. Even in the morning she was heavily made-up with pointless emphasis.—She wanted him to guess what she had in mind. "My, my," Fräulein Franziska crowed, "not much ingenuity." Then it came out: he would sing with her at "The Mud-hole." He was astounded and smiled in disbelief, but she explained the whole thing to him. He didn't really need much voice; after she had delivered the ballad of the bearded virgin, he would recite a poem, half to music—oh, she knew a charming poem, he'd be delighted—and then she would come on again from behind with her red scarf, and they would sing a duet together. As for this duet, Franziska related eagerly, well, thereby hung a tale— she had composed it herself. She stood and blushed mildly up to her wild, black hair. They must devote this week to rehearsal, that would be plenty. The beginning of next week was the first of the month exactly—October 1st—and before that they would come to some agreement with Alma Zeiserich. "And anyway," she suddenly said quite seriously and her eyes took on the clouded, yet scrutinizing look with which she had first examined him, "the singing doesn't matter so much— you've got good legs, and if you put on some makeup—" Their eyes met and held one another's gaze for a long while. They saw no cause to look away.

Paulchen dropped in and they became a threesome. Paulchen, who had on his best pink dressing gown, bubbled with delight. "We'll do it," he crowed again and again, "we'll paint your face!" Naturally Andreas had to appear as a sailor. Paulchen could even lay hands on a sailor's uniform. "It'll suit him better than me," said Paulchen and again the other youth felt grazed by that lackluster look that did not know what it meant. At that, Fräulein Franziska laughed coarsely, sitting at her dressing table.

Paulchen rapidly rattled off all the tittle-tattle about Alma Zeiserich. "I'm tellin' ya," he tittered, "she's been living off the same three songs for the last thirty years—honestly! that person! But the one about the potty's actually very clever!" he said and shook all over. He didn't need much, so he'd come right back from Herr Dorfbaum's.

* * *

They carried out all their schemes. Fräulein Franziska's energy guaranteed the consummation of so practical and necessary a venture.

They sought out Frau Zeiserich, whom they found in her low furnished lodgings for ladies. They settled on two weeks from the day. The wages were not very high, but otherwise adequate. "Besides, there are always perks," remarked the veteran manageress, as she bent over the contract at her desk. In other respects, she was remarkably hostile towards Andreas. "I really don't care for your type," she said and looked daggers at him. But as a partner of the treasured Franziska—and besides, she had a vacancy in the program.

Andreas had, meanwhile, grown accustomed to that look, he had even had it from the cabman and his unprepossessing mate. He met all these scrutinizing, appraising, hostilely evaluating looks with a smile not so much of defense, as a flat, winning reply, as if to say, "Yes—please—I do understand: naturally you have to put up with this sort of thing."

The evening came when Henriette carefully packed the sailor suit in Fräulein Franziska's bag, and Widow Meyerstein, laughing for no particular reason, wished he would break a leg. Barbara came home from her obscure daily outing, wearing a man's overcoat and a fedora tipped over her brow. She boisterously shook the beginner's right hand, as she stared steadily at Paulchen. Andreas also let Fräulein Anna wish him luck; he walked into her half-darkened room, where she sat in soot amid the bast- and metal-work and she turned her serene, broad face to him. "You going to work now?" she said—as if he were off to chop wood. "Lots of luck." And on his way out, Andreas considered that that might be the best way to do it. Fräulein Lisa, her eyes ablaze, hoped that his daemon would be well disposed, and only the old lady, only the grandmother said nothing, but watched him, perhaps staring a bit more than usual.—Henriette was silent too, as she gnawed her lips and looked at him. It was as if these two understood everything and found speech unnecessary.

The moment came when he waited between the black curtains until Fräulein Franziska had sung the severe and derisive moral to her ballad, walked back in bitter earnest wearing her red scarf, and left the space empty for him. She stood beside him for a moment, but said nothing, only scrutinized his face. But he philosophized momentarily as the M.C. outside announced that a charming young man from a prominent family would now present a couple of spicy bagatelles. "So the adventure is becoming reality—or is reality an adventure to begin with?"—and he failed to understand how he had suddenly made his entrance and, as the piano played an intro, was standing center stage. How the footlights glared. They hurt his eyes and he was afraid he would have to close them. Before him lay "The Mud-hole," red and round like a carousel, tastefully lit by subdued violet lamps. He could not make out anything specific. All he could see clearly and distinctly was Frau Zeiserich sitting in her box, a black cape thrown over her haughty brocade dress, so that the audience could not view in advance what it considered fantastic luxury. He noticed how thin her neck was and he also saw her marcelled hair. She for her part couldn't stand his type.

In time with the piano music, which ran riot, swelled and, trembling with emotion, calmed down again, he recited the song that Fräulein Franziska had suggested and rehearsed with him. His voice was husky, he felt as if he could never have the strength for the upswing the finale required. For at its finale, the poem, which began melancholically and cynically, boosted itself in an extravagant climax to an almost hymn-like thumping, a religiously gripping and yet somehow not very earnestly intended exaltation.

"Our legs are pretty, oh so pretty," his tentative, muffled voice began, and it shyly inquired of the red carousel, "Would you like to come our way? We're so alone, 'tis pity—All through the livelong day."

Someone below said out loud, "Come along then—." Andreas heard him and looked down at the floor. He also heard the clattering of the forks, nor did he fail to catch the gentle gurgle of the wine pouring out of bottles. His senses, though painfully acute, were totally confused. But he surrendered himself and, there, on the little stage, went on with the story.

> Our bed is warm and cosy,
> We dream of lust and blood.
> Our small home town was nosy,
> And so we left for good.

At this last line he tossed his head back a bit. The rhythm of the song, the fascinating tempo he loved: here it came, now he got into it. Let the crowd out there with its beefsteaks scoff. He knew that it wasn't the crowning glory of literature. But it was subtitled, "A Street Song." And now the piano called to him compellingly, imperiously. Forgetting about the subject matter, he cried to the public in a voice whose hoarseness suddenly vanished:

> So now we pace the district,
> A red scarf round our throat,
> We prowl about the district,
> And we don't give a hoot.

And pretty soon we'll die now,
You can't live long this way,
We'll croak and say goodbye now,
See you on Judgment Day—"

Concentrated now, giving his all to portray the great
punishment and the great compassion with his voice:

We all approach God's holy throne,
His brow so black with threat,
We bow before His only Son,—
But mad he doesn't get.

It's not our fault, that's understood,
We're so alone, 'tis pity—
We left for good, we left for good—
Our legs are oh, so pretty.—

How thin his voice had become at the finale. The last words
came very succinctly, dead tired, conclusive, that mention of
the legs imploring for help. The exhausted voice really
sounded as if they and their beauty had been the reason for it
all.—But his voice had done it well.

The applause was scanty, quite painfully sparse. They had
found the street song far too cynical in contrast to Alma's
boisterous potty number.

Fräulein Franziska was suddenly beside him in her apache
gear. Her black hair stood out wild and tangled around her
severe face. Now came their ensemble piece, their wonderful
duet. They had rehearsed it very carefully. Fräulein Franziska
had kept things on target. It was rather an odd musical skit, a
moving, indeed despairing parley between this apache girl and
the sailor with the painted face. It ended with her dancing
around him, up and down the whole stage, stamping her feet
and flinging her arms, her skirts caught up, with gallows
humor, anger and passion in her mottled face, while he stood

in the center, his cap tipped low over his brow, his eyes closed, and clapped in time to it. It was a genuine climax when, with a ghastly shriek and disheveled hair, she threw herself at his feet.

This crass sketch of underworld life had been arranged so morbidly and so effectively that it was much more to the taste of "The Mud-hole's" audience. The applause was cordial, and as Andreas was sitting in his cubbyhole of a dressing room taking off his make-up, Fräulein Zeiserich walked right in and said, derogatorily as ever—ah, there no mistaking what the sparse applause had meant—"Go on out again and show your shopworn beauty to the gentlemen—you hear, they're mad about you—" And out he went, submissive to every command, saw the carousel again before his weary eyes, heard the applause which meant nothing more than a stupid racket, stood there in his sailor suit and bowed to them sitting over their red wine. But Paulchen, very slim and fragile in his lilac silk outfit, was standing in the wings, looking at him. He blinked feebly and his lips whispered expressively: "It was divine—you did it delightfully—," stood amid the flats, winked, smiled, whispered, as if he were quite out of his mind.

As Andreas was back sitting in his dressing room, he had to press his brow to the mirror. So that was his face. The woman who lived off of three vulgar songs and a cheap glittering brocade dress had called his beauty "shopworn." And he felt as if he himself could see traces of premature decay around that artificially blood-red mouth, whose artificiality blotched everything it touched, and around these cheeks, made up far too white. Shopworn? But wasn't the lady right?—His eyes gazed morbidly out of the darkened rims which Fräulein Franziska had painted around them with careful hand.—"What is our generation really after?" he heard the girl's voice ask. But as always, when things were at their worst, the smile triumphed in that face once more, implying that somehow it knew better. Oh, sweet danger, said the smile to that face, oh, mysterious

risk—pious hope of enlightenment—most blessed, most esoteric awareness that enlightenment is at hand—

And that night he got drunk somewhere noisy. Where the
jazz music piped and shrieked, where tarts plied their voluptu-
ous charms in little side-boxes, Andreas sat with strange
people, his face veiled by cigarette smoke, and smiled and
talked nonsense in which he eventually got lost, babbled in
bewilderment and drank.

But when he got home that night, he found a little prickly
cactus standing on his night table. Beside it lay an ordinary
pink card. "From Henriette. With heartfelt wishes for success
on your opening night."—His sense inebriated, he stared,
mute and suddenly incapable of movement, at this timorous
yet prickly homage from that pinched heart.

***

The second time he sang, Alma Zeiserich poked her skinny
face into his little dressing room where he sat half-dressed
before the mirror, too tired to take off his make-up. "A
gentleman is interested in you," she said impudently through
the chink in the door and twisted her ugly mouth. "I suppose
you'd like me to show him in—"

The gentleman appeared to have been standing directly
behind her. Hardly had she withdrawn when, fat and well-
groomed, he strode into the cubbyhole. His screwed-in
monocle looked round sourly, for the room was chockful of
clothes and make-up and cigarette butts. But then that
distressed mouth was smiling and chattering in a Viennese
accent. "Dorfbaum's the name. I'm a writer, actually."

Andreas didn't understand why he said "actually." Turned
halfway towards his guest as he sat before his greasy dressing
table, he had become as white as the plaster wall he faced.
"Yes," was all he said, and no further word issued from his lips.

But the well-groomed Herr Dorfbaum, smiling and blinking close behind him—he was even holding a nosegay of violets, Andreas noticed for the first time—Herr Dorfbaum said graciously and directly into his neck, "Well, you sang that very comically—really most amusing—"

And Andreas replied, still white in the face, a lump in his throat, his whole body trembling: "Perhaps you'd like to take a seat?"

Although his voice nearly failed him—he nevertheless made a rather peculiar, but adroit gesture with his hand, like someone wandering in a trance, and, eyes averted, indicated the only chair available.

5

Berlin was big.

Although Andreas hated it with every fiber of his being, had indeed abhorred it from the very morning it had afflicted him with its merciless ugliness, quite like a nightmare vision—nevertheless every day and every night he wanted to circulate in it again, full of reverence and humility, in its unfathomable, mysterious, inexhaustible magnitude.

He aimed no accusations at its destructiveness, he uttered no reproaches at the filth that made so many believe they had to forecast its catastrophic end. He merely walked around and looked—for there were so many people living there, wearing themselves out and striving to find themselves—some, who went on doing their little bits of work every day and thought good hard labor was enough for them, and others, who exhausted themselves extravagantly with the ambitious thought that they would accomplish something extraordinary, even crucial, and went around desperately talkative or doggedly mute and would probably have to lay down their wretched arms some day for all that. Or still others who had already fallen by the wayside—perhaps without even a prior struggle—and whom men called "the lost." Andreas came in contact with

69

so many of them. Some held his attention for a greater time, some a lesser. He met them on the street or in cafés or Meyerstein's boarding house, where they came to call on somebody or other. He spoke with them, looked at them, hoped they would enable him to become clever.

The young people who were looking for Anna, who sat busy and begrimed over her work, were homely and diligent, indeed, diligent in quite a monastic and impassioned way. They dressed unconventionally, in linen cowls and ample waterproof woollen overcoats. Their eyes were opaque but warm and their footfalls heavy.

Fräulein Barbara had many visitors as well, but they were a wholly different type. She herself was basically a kind-hearted child, but she loved young stockbrokers who wore short fur walking coats, laughed contemptuously through their noses when the talk turned to art and literature, and preferred to boast about their elegant and hypothetical sportsmanship, which was of exclusive interest to them.

On the other hand, darkly dressed, priest-like, arrogant persons went in and out of Fräulein Lisa's, the artisan's: spiritual ladies, buttoned-up adolescents with sidelong glances. Andreas knew they were intitiates of that arcane philosophico-religious sect, who moved about wanly and knew it all. But Andreas could stand them the least. He found everyone unappealing who arrogantly believed he had found a way out, when all he had found was a dead end.—In opposition to that he genuinely preferred Paulchen, who was stupid to the point of imbecility, but in whose milky face the thin dismal little lines of sorrow carved themselves ever deeper around his mouth.— And Andreas thought he knew why.

Andreas walked amidst them all, listening, looking, full of humility and curiously adroit, like someone wandering in a trance.

How big Berlin was by day. Andreas could not make out

what it created, why anyone would live and suffer there. But he breathed it in the air, he inhaled it and it made his heart beat faster.

He looked at the children who, ugly and sallow like his little friend Henriette, played in the garbage behind wooden palings, and they terrified him, for each one, scrawny and innocent, was growing up to meet his own mysterious fate, his own guilt. And the boys who walked to school earnestly and silently in grown-up's clothing, already held their personal question in their eyes.—He looked into the face of every passerby and read in each one a new adventure. He even listened to the cold noises of the street, which were apparently impassive, penetrating and merciless; but he, an attentive and grateful child, moved through them and hugged them to him as a great song of humanity.

But how much bigger the city was by night, when it instantly enlarged into a gigantic blazing dream which, suddenly, through the supreme ruthless will of some god had to become flesh-and-blood, a reality capable of suffering. How big the city stood above the masses, when the evening ignited the dissolute splendor of its electric signs, the illuminations circling and flaring off and on like a great festival, when, pragmatic and intoxicated at the same time, it lay like a beast burning in passion at the feet of God.

Then, after he had sung at "The Mud-hole," Andreas was glad to move through all the streets, pale in his bright camel's hair coat, and Paulchen and Fräulein Franziska went with him.

They said little, did the three. Franziska, the dark red hat tipped down over her brow, squinted her black eyes dimly into the distance or sometimes cast a sidelong glance back at Andreas. Pale Paulchen tripped along in his bright yellow shoes, a lilac silk handkerchief in the breast pocket of his ladylike overcoat, the carefully painted mouth anxiously pursed.—Andreas walked between them, usually bareheaded, his eyes hooded.

Yellowish gray and stretching out into the distance, a rapid string of motor cars slipped by them. Between the black of the night and the raging yellow of the electric signs strutted the old tarts, crossly talking business to one another, shriveled and mottled like mummies in their shabby furs and down-at-heel red ankle-boots. But the husky voices of the news vendors, painfully cracked and overtopping one another, resounded as if Error and Fashion, yammering a mysteriously discordant magic spell and loudly complaining, were trying to narrate the legends of this city.

Andreas liked it best when, on such evenings, Franziska made the modest proposal that they look for one of the "appropriate" nightclubs.

In the vicinity of the main streets, though at a decent remove, naturally, there was some of what they were seeking, and, for all that, it managed to show a bit of its elegance: places where queerly heightened merriment prevailed and youths in alluring outfits tossed paper streamers into the air. With ladylike charm, the landlord, white, fat and heavily perfumed, would shout out a welcome to them. The young gentlemen would burst into shrill notes of rejoicing whenever such old acquaintances as Andreas, Paul and Franziska dropped by the club; their hands made small darting movements as if they were tossing their dear guests flowers or little balls of silk; they would call, "Hello, sunshine! Just look, the three Graces!"— and shake like dancers on the high, uncomfortable barstools they used as perches. But soon they would come over to the threesome's table, for they knew them to be well-disposed, first to joke a little, to make a great fuss over a silk train which, as the great ladies they were now, they pretended to wear, to get tipsy on the wine they were treated to. Then their eyes would suddenly grow earnest, their carefully painted faces would collapse beneath the layer of cosmetics, they would sit down, this time with very unaffected movements, and begin to talk about money.

The conversation would soon become sharply focused. Paulchen, basically very much one of their kind, wanted exact information about their earnings, and had to find out how much this one or that one had paid. In very quiet, bashful voices they would supply the information. Their faces were so gentle, if only one looked at them closely enough, gentle faces with lackluster eyes. Andreas looked at them more closely. He found that they all reminded him a bit of Paulchen. They all had the same look and he also recognized the dismal lines around their mouths. In each case, it was a different fate that had carved them there. None of them was doing very well.

While motherly Fräulein Franziska sat among a group of youths and shrewdly reckoned up approximately how much money she might give to one or another who was particularly needy, Paulchen, his head propped up and his eyes filled with mild excitement, would trade gossip with his former colleagues. "I'm tellin' ya," he would whisper and arch his eyebrows high in amazement, "that Herr Dorfbaum—honestly, that fat Herr Dorfbaum!—" Then suddenly, breaking off almost in delight, he would heartily clap his interlocutor on the shoulder. "Oh, you know," he would say, "we're just a couple of crazy queens!" And the young man to whom he had laughed his confession rejoiced with him. They all laughed, those at the bar and on the dance floor as well, where they held one another in lopsided embraces and stepped deftly to the music. They raised their champagne glasses and tumblers of lemonade, the whole club drank to each other, all the artistically groomed faces laughing together, non-stop, as if oddly united in a profound understanding.—Paulchen's face with its milky skin would become serious again. The laughter would cease, they would sit there once more with despairing eyes and talk about their poverty.

Of all these clubs, Andreas best loved the "Little Garden of Eden" on the first floor of an elegant house; you walked up a mouldy red staircase to be greeted upstairs with a particularly teasing shout of joy. "Rosepetal" was to be found here, aging but still slender as a fir tree. Although a withering had set in around his mouth and cheeks, he danced just as dexterously and carried his curly auburn head just as charmingly as a diva in an operetta. He would hold his perfumed hanky under Andreas's nose and crow, "Quick, quick—my intended!" and poked him menacingly with his ring-bedecked finger.—In one corner sat little Boris, gentle and stupefied by the narcotic to which he was addicted, his delicate face wearily propped up, his eyes pathetically bedimmed from within. Then Andreas would sit down beside him, while Paulchen danced with Rosepetal, and would speak with him quietly. Boris focused his nearly blind eyes—it seemed as if they would never see anything again—on his only friend, who always came and asked how he was—and he would say: "Thanks, things are all right—my landlady wants to evict me—thanks for asking—" How touching was the fleeting and sorrowful smile with which he took the money Andreas gave him.—Meanwhile the short dark-haired gentleman in the tuxedo would appear on the dance floor, greeted by extravagantly jubilant applause, would put one hand gracefully on his hip and sing his little song. "If you want to get a lover, you must stroll down Tauentzien—" And the young hustlers tapped their patent-leather shoes in time with the music. But Boris, alone at his table, would turn halfway to the wall and hurriedly take a pinch of that fine white stuff that looks as appetizing as snuff and is as cool in the nose as peppermint—and in the end has the same effect.

When the night was further advanced, when it had gone two or three o'clock, they would travel out into the desolate districts of the city, down by the river, where the gas lamps dimly flared. They would stop by "Saint Margaret's Cellar" and be greeted heartily there too. But here the heartiness was more hollow, less effervescent, not so buoyantly maintained as up west. The room, down a couple of steps, was cramped and the air so thick that it was hard to breathe. The deaf, stocky landlord with the drooping white mustache would walk back and forth, stroking the boys' hair with morose affection when they pleased him, swatting them when they annoyed him.

What the piano was hammering out was hard to tell, but Paulchen was already dancing in the middle of the room with a black man, who leaned back his big woolly head and yielded to the movement with barbaric sentimentality; he held up his little partner's big face with its blood-red lips pouting as if to be kissed. While Andreas was transacting important business with a savage-looking sailor who, pipe in mouth and blond hair over his dirty forehead, was trying to clarify the details in a North German dialect, Fräulein Franziska sat all alone by the wall, as anomalous as a mask.

The transvestites began to quarrel. They got up—tall youths in women's clothes—angrily at their table, their raucous voices clamored and squalled beneath their black silk hats. The mustachioed landlord skillfully interposed and even hit one of the ladies square in the face, so that she had to bleed into her big, blue-checked scarf.—The black disappeared provocatively into the toilet. A teen-aged youth sat down by Fräulein Franziska, his ravaged child's face was unwashed, but he immediately assumed that Fräulein Franziska was a man in woman's clothing and asked, his face averted suddenly with a last vestige of shame, whether the gentleman was already set up for the evening. Another man, alone at his wooden table, had fallen asleep before his beer. He snored loudly, his head supported on his arms.

The air was so thick that it was very hard to breathe. But Andreas sat silently at the bar, where the decrepit wife of the mustachioed man sold schnapps,—sat silently and breathed it in. Beyond, almost in the back of the room, lay Paulchen, his mouth pursed anxiously, already half in the arms of the eager black. The transvestites were preparing to leave, embarrassed by handbags and encumbered by umbrellas. Simultaneously they threatened the landlord with a summons and hurried in tandem to the door. Fräulein Franziska looked in her purse to see if she had anything left for the fifteen-year-old, who had taken her for an "admirer," and found a little small change. Earnestly and minutely she searched and the dirty child watched her every movement with great anxiety.

Andreas suddenly realized that little Boris was still sitting in the "Little Garden of Eden," fragile and stupefied—waiting for someone to pick him up. The thought gripped his heart so abruptly that he thought he would have to spring from his seat. He sat down by Franziska and stroked the much-neglected hair of the fifteen-year-old. "What's your name?" he said as he bent over him, and suddenly felt Fräulein Franziska raise her earnest, fixed, questioning gaze to him. The youngster said, "Hans"—and nothing more. But Franziska added, as if in explanation, "Of course he has nowhere at all to stay—" and she did not remove her black eyes from Andreas, who failed to understand her obscure remark. He merely smoothed down the child's hair and the thoughts in his heart became veiled and light. "I once dreamed," he thought even as he stroked, "that the consecration of great innocence would come upon me during the course I have adopted. Now I almost know how it will come to pass."—

The door upstairs was opened again. A clean-shaven actor in a fur coat came in, to find himself something for the night. The street noises clanged remotely. The husky voices of the news vendors could still be heard, very far away. Even now they were narrating the legends of this city—in magic spells which no one understood—far away—at the ends of the earth.

The black had disappeared somewhere with Paulchen.

Franziska sat as only women know how to sit, serene, patient, a complicitous little smile on her lips. She sat and looked at Andreas.

But he stroked and thought. He only stroked and thought.

6

Andreas had to do with some exceptionally queer characters in the course of an evening. This city contained some peculiar gentlemen.

It turned out that down there in the circular carousel of "The Mud-hole" there were those who heeded more than his legs; this made-up young man seemed to prompt a certain pedagogical interest as well. No one knew whether such interest was aroused by his helpless, put-upon charm, his somehow imperiled, already damaged beauty, or whether they attended to the dejected, impassioned text of his poem with the thought that there must be something more to its speaker. Many felt the need to help, many the desire to "rescue" one who looked about to go under. They came to him and talked, they lay hands on him, warned him, affectionately pointed out the danger his vulnerability was running. He never contradicted, gave a great deal of thought to what they said, listened to them earnestly and considerately, took it to heart, and in many instances granted that they were right. But in the end they all ran aground on his mysterious boyish little smile that suggested, in spite of it all, that he "knew better."

Whenever he sat before the mirror in the cubbyhole of a dressing room, busy with cold cream and powder, at every opportunity Frau Zeiserich would stretch her skinny female neck through the crack in the door and hiss: "Yet another gentleman for our Andreas—I don't suppose you'll want to receive him—"

The hardest fight was with the man with the black, wildly

upstanding hair and the incandescent eyes. He talked coolly and correctly in the ghastly calm before the storm: "Excuse me for disturbing you—," he bowed and his large mouth twitched with nervousness. "I happened to be in this club inadvertently" he said and stared around not so much in disgust as in anger. "An acquaintance had enticed me here and it interested me, for the sake of research." He was badly dressed, Andreas noticed, his boots were rough; he had crossed his legs, and the boot on the dangling foot hung as heavily as an iron weight. "But I noticed at once: you don't belong here!" he went on. His words were sharply accentuated, vibrating in their fervent tension. "You are a young man and must have got into this ignoble situation quite by accident." He bent back his large head, whose black, stiff hair stood up like a militant halo, almost closed his eyes and spoke very quietly but as passionately in inflexion as if such a whisper were more intense than any roaring could be. "I assume that you are entirely heedless of your actions and their consequences. You stand out there on a tawdry red stage and do a little playacting. You make a fool of yourself for a company of profiteers and parasites on civilization. No one takes you seriously. They jeer at you, asking whether you're keen on having an affair, doing a little erotic moonlighting, even whether it's part of your job. That may possibly be the case—for all I care. But you are a respectable youth, I see it in your eyes and in each of your movements. You are certainly weak-willed, but intelligent. Your body loves lechery and self-degradation, but you have a defense in your heart.—I do not suppose that the art you practice as best you can in this mud-hole is the only one you pursue. At home you paint or write a bit of poetry. So far these domestic efforts of yours have gone unnoticed. In a couple of years, you may put them before the public and even win applause for them: nothing in your situation will have changed on that account. You will remain the fool, the plaything not to be taken seriously by a blasé, useless bourgeoisie, and you will have to be destroyed along with it."

He stood up, stocky in build but his face ablaze as he moved to the middle to the room. He raised his fists, quaking as he spoke to Andreas: "Young people must realize that nowadays art has nothing to do with it, art is becoming irrelevant. The whole bourgeoisie has been fooling itself for years with its unparalleled frivolity, overlooking the fact that the only question that is basically worth discussing today is the social question. The bourgeoisie does not seem to sense that in ten or at most twenty years a catastrophe of the most monstrous kind will befall it and its antiquated civilization, if this question, this one question is not solved beforehand.—But it delights in refined chamber music, pretty landscapes, adores ethical novels, while the catastrophe comes inexorably closer!" He had been taking broad strides back and forth in his contempt, but now he sat down again. Andreas only listened, pale in the face. "I have founded an organization for young men," said the man in the chair, "who passionately agree that salvation is to be hoped for only by this means. My friends range in age from fifteen to twenty. They work by day in factories or construction sites. We are all bound together by friendship and love, which the bourgeoisie we so hate might perhaps deem immoral."

With glowing eyes and eloquent lips, he walked over to Andreas and stood at his side. He bent over him and put both arms around his shoulders. He pulled the boy to him, so that Andreas felt both the pain of a throttling and the comfort of a great embrace. "From the first moment I saw you," the man said, twitching into this young, white, impenetrable face, "I knew that you must belong to our circle. Do you understand what I mean? Do you now understand our aim?"—and Andreas merely nodded, while the voices and thoughts inside him clashed and crushed one another. "Yes—I do understand—." "We want to stick together—until the great day comes," the hot voice above him whispered, "wait together in love, create together in love, until the great day is here." The arms clasped him even more tightly. "Come!" urged the voice.

But suddenly Andreas replied, and did not know why, "I cannot." "Why not?" asked the man leaning over him, "why can't you? Have you heard nothing of what I was saying to you? You were sitting there so silently—didn't you understand?! Did no word get through to you?!"—Then the child's face beneath him smiled: "Indeed I did understand everything you said—thanks for everything—but I cannot join—"

The man released him, went from him to the door. "Then there's no help possible for you," he said, his great head drooping. His voice was weaker and darkness passed over his brow like a cloud.

"Greet your friends for me!" said the boy before the mirror. The man replied, "Thanks. We shall all have you in our thoughts." "So long then," said the youth. And the man replied, "So long—yes—I'll greet my friends for you—so long, my child—"

* * *

Later Paulchen came quietly into the dressing room.

"You had a visitor?" he asked suspiciously. "Was there a guy here again?" "Yes," said Andreas, "an old friend—"

"You've got such a way with people," said Paulchen and smiled somewhat wearily. "You going home now?" "No," said Andreas, leaning dead tired against the wall. "I'm still going out—" But Paulchen had his own opinion and anxiously raised a hand in admonition: "You go out too much—you really do go out too much—so do I, by the way," he added and cast down his lackluster gaze, as if in shame.

* * *

Although a snob by nature and passionately devoted to gossip about the upper classes, Doctor Dorfbaum had serious intentions towards Andreas. He received him in his rose-red quilted dressing gown with a racy little anecdote. "Say, do you know Countess Donnerstal?" he asked giddily. "Well, in the first place, she is definitely not a countess—"

His apartment had very low cramped rooms, but was richly, indeed luxuriously furnished with silken cushions and lampshades. Dainty knick-knacks stood around as in a lady's boudoir. One drank orange liqueur out of miniature silver goblets. Dorfbaum told funny stories about Count Pritzle-witz.—

But a great change occurred over the course of the evening. Dorfbaum's fat face grew troubled, his little eyes shone with desire, and he complained. "I don't understand you," he noised to Andreas's face. "I cannot figure out your silence. And yet you must feel how serious I am about this. I'll do whatever you want." Helplessly he wrung his little hands. "I'll give you money," he said quietly and shook his head in despair. "You sit there every bit as alien as you were the first day. And yet you must feel how serious I am about this."

But Andreas consoled him quietly and with averted eyes. "Don't worry," he said, "it won't last—"

Doctor Dorfbaum would accept no consolation. "Maybe it's the generation gap," he wailed in his dressing gown, "maybe you're all inaccessible to us. You lack a certain something we had as young people—a tenderness, a sense of style. For all your sensitivity, you're hard. But it must be lovely to be loved—"

Then Andreas said, very gruffly, turned towards the shadows—Doctor Dorfbaum did not entirely understand his words: "I do not believe what you say—you are essentially indifferent to me—no one loves me. *Being* loved doesn't matter. I am as alone as a beast."

One morning—it was still rather early and nearly everyone was asleep—something very nasty happened.

A sharp scolding dialogue suddenly began in the corridor. One could recognize the rather husky voice of Fräulein Barbara, and a gentleman's voice crying bloody murder in reply. "Under no conditions!" Barbara shouted—and one could clearly hear her stamp her foot—"do what you want—I won't come with you!" "You refuse?" shrieked the gentleman in so rhetorically strident a counter question that his voice cracked and broke on the highest note, "then I see I'm obliged to use force!" And the crash of the word "Force" filled the whole lodging house, as if someone had smashed a china service on the floor.

Fräulein Barbara laughed—in a very coarse bass voice. Now he grabbed her wrist, one could hear the racket of the grappling and contending. "Let go of me," gasped Barbara— how quickly her laughter had died away—"go away—do what you can—"

Everyone who was eavesdropping at his door or, waked out of sleep by the racket, intently listening, sitting up in bed, head propped up, had long since realized what was going on. Barbara's foster father, the short, rich and choleric gentleman who had adopted the ill-bred girl as a baby and brought her up in his palatial house in Nuremberg, had finally shown up, knew her address, had, in spite of everything, learned her hiding place, her little bolt-hole, and was there to take her, send her back home without standing on ceremony. "Let me go," Barbara gasped. But he yanked her by the wrist.—The others eavesdropped from their rooms.

Then an awful noise was heard. There was a loud rumble, a stifled cry, and someone dropped on to the floor.

They came out of every doorway, faces appeared on all sides, eager to see what had happened. What was going on?— Oh woeful sight—there lay Barbara's father, the gentleman who had spent so much money on her upbringing, crumpled on the carpet, his bowler hat a few feet away from him. As he had tried to yank her by the wrist, his daughter must have shaken him off so furiously and given him such a push that, panting, he had crashed against the wall and onto the floor. Blood ran thickly from his nose and over the tiles in a turbid trickle. His hands, in their brown leather gloves, swam in blood. After all, his daughter was so big and strong—

Sleepy faces with wide-awake eyes were in all the doorways. Andreas's face did not flinch, motionless and seemingly paralyzed for a few seconds in the black opening of his door, then it turned away, never taking its eyes off the bleeding father, and disappeared back into his room. But Fräulein Lisa's face, pale and astonished in its excitement, had hot, frightened eyes. Paulchen's face was filled with a pallid, uncomprehending fear, the eyes and eyebrows were arched high in the same way as when they discoursed on Herr Dorfbaum's way of life.—More faces appeared in many corners. It was like a mask shop where suddenly, after everything has been cleared away, the many motley masks are hung out and presented for inspection in their bizarre variety. Fräulein Franziska's black eyes, which could never be surprised by anything any more and therefore took a vague interest in everything, stared darkly—curiously—from beneath her upstanding hair.—Henriette's pinched visage emerged from somewhere, cunning and narrow in a corner.— With blue cheeks and brushed hair the grandmother's large head towered up out of the sitting room. Fräulein Anna's clay-yellow Hindu face looked silent and broad out of the background.—Thank God the widow herself was not there, but out shopping. With what ghastly energy she would have intervened.

But Barbara leaned against the wall, her face buried in her arms, in the same position that had repelled her insistent father. She wept in a gurgling, gulping way, shaking the vast, fat body beneath the dressing gown.

Very slowly, moaning, her father sorted himself out. He pulled out a large white silk handkerchief and let his turbid blood flow into it. Stooping, his nose buried in his handkerchief, he stumbled to the door. Near the door, however, he had to stoop again, to collect his dusty little hat. That hurt—his bones ached so much. And suddenly—perhaps in raging vexation at this new affliction—he shook his skinny ruddy fist, shook it trembling at his child, at all young people, at the whole boarding house.—Then he slammed the door behind him.

Fräulein Barbara, still sobbing against the cold wall, had not observed this last, convulsive miming of a vengeful oath. But when the door slammed with explosive noise, she stirred as if whipped, and her sobs became spasms that shook her and doubled her up.

With hunched shoulders and a mouth tightly pursed in anxiety, Paulchen in his yellow silk outfit walked quietly over to her, and smoothly stroked the length of her quivering back with his light hands. "Fatty," he said, "Be a good girl, Fatty—there, there, there—let's be nice and quiet—"

Barbara turned her face, an overgrown child's face, dissolved in tears, melting, the eyes desperate, towards him. She howled convulsively at her anguished comforter, weeping miserably. "It can't really be true," she lamented in ringing tones, "I can't believe it's true—it must have been a dream—" And she wept to this white empty face she so loved, the face that confronted her in its meticulous milkiness and knew no other comfort than this helpless: "There, there, there—"

* * *

"This city is a strain," Andreas said later to his friend Franziska, as she sat idly amid the disorder of her room. "I almost get scared when I see my face in the mirror. The cheekbones stand out so clearly—." Thoughtfully he puffed out the cigarette smoke. How rapidly one got used to these pungent little things here, something seemed to be missing when one did not have their facile stimulus between one's fingers, their charming smoke before one's face. Still, one ought to be glad not to need sniffs of the appetizing white powder. "It's a strain," he repeated, shaking his head in the smoke, as though surprised that his indefatigable inquisitiveness was showing signs of exhaustion.

But Fräulein Franziska, strumming on her lute, said slowly, as if she were reciting her modest text to a bleary melody: "Alma Zeiserich is giving us a vacation—we'll go to the country, Andreas, we'll go to the country together. I have a friend in Central Germany, her name is Frau Privy Councilor Gartner—we'll pay a visit to her villa—we'll spend a few days with her."

And as she spoke, she stroked Andreas's hands. Her hands felt rough, although she had long manicured fingernails that glowed pink as if they were lacquered.—But her hands— broad hands with strong bones and rather long fingers—had lost their smoothness.

They wanted to relax together, as far as they could.

* * *

That very afternoon they were on the train. Fräulein Franziska in a very practical gray traveling outfit had laid her head peacefully against the carriage window. But Andreas offered his face to the passing landscape and the wind. "Train travel is lovely," he said, half turned back to her—but the wind still held his hair in its grip.

And she replied, as if this were the only possible answer: "At my friend's place you'll meet Niels too—I believe she's adopted him—" And she smiled from her padded seat, as if she knew everything in advance.

THREE

1

F RAU Privy Councilor Gartner lived in an old cloister that had once been part of a convent and was picturesquely situated overlooking the river.

During their ride in a one-horse shay through the little university town and, later, along the river, Fräulein Franziska related her friend's early life circumstantially and impartially, as was her way. In younger days—if one lent credence to Fräulein Franziska's earnest narrative—she had led the most dissolute life under the name of Gertrud von Trautening. She had been celebrated as a star and a prodigy in operetta, beloved, even deified in Paris, London and New York. She had even ventured onto the grand opera stage, though without such an enthusiastic response. "But her greatest triumphs were achieved in the bedroom," Fräulein Franziska declared darkly.

The river coiled through the rather smooth, undulating beauty of the countryside. A mountain ruin beckoned picturesquely, indeed flirtatiously from every hilltop. But the leaves on the trees now bore a yellowish tint.—Andreas only half heeded the romance that Fräulein Franziska was doing her best to spin at his side. The Indian summer atmosphere transfigured the trees and everything else. The air shivered and shimmered in its blue serenity.

"At the age of thirty-eight Gertrud married Privy Councilor Gartner, because she was feeling burnt out," the slow, coarse voice reported. "He was an outstanding crackpot. Although very rich, he wanted to produce an unlimited supply of gold, and to this end he had a remarkable alchemical laboratory set up in an old convent he had acquired from a bankrupt count. Gertrud, whose beauty had driven him to frenzy, he treated with kid gloves until he passed away after a single year of wedlock. I have never doubted that the councilor's wife had a hand in the matter."

They climbed up a steep lane bordered with fruit trees; now they could see the gray gate of the convent garden above their heads. A stark madonna peered out behind the branches of the apple trees. "I was a close friend of Gertrud's for years," Franziska said and stared straight ahead. "I believe we felt that, in many ways, we could always rely on one another. Now that she's living in the convent, she often invites me to visit. You shall see how beautiful she is.—I have always felt sorry that she never had a child, either by the privy councilor or by one of her friends. Now she's centered all her pedagogical passion on this Niels, whom she spoils utterly. I don't know where it will all end."

On the crunching gravel path they crossed the park, where the tall red beeches formed a mysterious covert. A turkeycock strutted malignantly in the gloaming. A chained dog with yellow eyes barked and howled in impotent rage. Tall, blue, rather sallow flowers throve on either side. Amid the enchanted movement of the convent garden Fräulein Franziska said, "These days, so I've heard, she's proceeding with the crazy plan of adopting the young man."

The convent itself lay low and outspread among the trees;

it looked gray and dilapidated, and only the large windows shone and shimmered like the most delicate crystal.

A swarthy, dumpy retainer opened the carriage door for them. He had a glass eye, but the living one was all the more intense and dark in comparison. Fräulein Franziska knew him of old; he bowed obsequiously and eagerly led them through many cool passages, still reeking with damp, to their rooms which were next to one another. "The mistress hopes to see the lady and gentleman at tea on the veranda," he said as he opened the doors and fussily arranged their valises.

Andreas's room was small, severe and elegantly furnished. The pale brown furniture had long spindly legs suggesting that anyone who sat on it would be sure to break it. A Botticelli Madonna stared sweet and childlike from the wall.

Andreas walked over to the window. His view was over the river. In his heart he felt a happiness he could not understand as he breathed in deeply the pure air of this landscape.

* * *

Downstairs on the terrace the privy councilor's widow was awaiting her guests behind a silver tea service. She rose and held out her beringed hand to Fräulein Franziska. "How good of you to come!" she said and her voice was beautiful, but strikingly lifeless, with a metallic, almost tinny clang to it. Fräulein Franziska looked darkly at her friend and introduced Andreas Magnus. The councilor's wife was mildly friendly to him and she glanced at him coyly from beneath her eyelids, her cheeks dimpled, and she said, he must be about Niels's age.— There was, in addition, a sprightly little man with a big nose and bright eyes. "Doctor Zäuberlin," said the councilor's wife, "my foster son's tutor—"

As they sat down, Fräulein Franziska slowly asked where Niels was. But Frau Gartner replied somewhat hastily, as she poured the tea, "He must be in the garden—or out for a walk—."

They could look out over the river, where the skiffs were gliding. Students in white pullovers were training for a race.

The tea table conversation concerned the old convent and its unique atmosphere. Doctor Zäuberlin did most of the talking, in a somewhat aggressive, indeed grotesque way. His gallantry to the ladies was stylized and courtly in a medieval fashion. "Do have some, my dearest lady," he would say and held out the dainty sugar bowl to Fräulein Franziska, who was examining him through and through. In addressing the councilor's wife, he lowered his darting mouse eyes. "Kind lady—," he said, and his voice trailed off with a troubadour's servility.

The talk soon shifted from architecture and ancient civilization to Niels, for the councilor's wife would not have it otherwise. "I am trying so hard to educate Niels a little in all these things," she said in her bell-like voice, "or rather I invite Doctor Zäuberlin to come every day and do whatever he can for his education, for I don't know a great deal myself—" "The councilor's wife knows more than we do about everything," Doctor Zäuberlin said quietly, but he articulated overemphatically as he bent his bird's face with its jagged mouth more deeply over his dish. Still the councilor's wife went on as if this were an important addendum to the matter, "Doctor Zäuberlin was a friend of my late husband. They worked together in the laboratory—"

Andreas could see that the councilor's wife was still beautiful. She retained the wonderfully symmetrical, rather buxom female form which, twenty years earlier, had been the ideal of the aesthetes. Her profile was noble and Grecian and her blue-gray eyes shone, although their shimmer contained something of the emptiness and lifelessness that made her melodious voice metallic. But by far the most beautiful thing was her auburn hair, which she wore in thick braids plaited around her head, so that it crowned her richly like a precious diadem.

"We don't let him learn anything irrelevant," she said and shook her head helplessly, "or read anything boring or work on more than a little mathematics. I mean for him to obtain a little general knowledge, I only want to help him, he is a child in jeopardy."

Andreas suddenly saw how she might once have stood, adorned with drooping ostrich plumes, in an operetta theatre, as the One and Only, the Star of Stars, before a line of envious chorus-girls. The audience rejoiced and tossed roses at her. In the wings, her lover, her gallant, her lieutenant was waiting. The last strains of her wonderful voice echoed and dissolved in a breathtaking way over the stalls like the gold and silver balls she was lavishly scattering and distributing. The celebrated woman raised her arms in ecstatic, hard-edged frivolity. White silk swam about her body. The giant halo of plumes swayed over her merry face.

Now she was saying—and her mouth twitched touchingly—: "Basically he is perfectly incorrigible. He stays away all day, I don't know with whom, and all our efforts are in vain.— Forgive me for talking about things that don't matter to you," she suddenly addressed Andreas, and the dimples broke out on her face, slight vestiges of a once expert coquetry, "but after all you are his contemporary—"

A voice called from out of the bushes. It was very clear and yet a bit husky, glowing with an unspeakably acrid sheen. It called, "Gertrud—listen, Gertrud!"—and the lady at the tea table looked up, as she suddenly folded her white beringed hands on the tablecloth. "Yes," her voice answered, its metallic lifelessness touchingly coming to life. "Yes, yes!"—And the other voice replied from the garden: "Do you have guests?— Then bring them into the garden—down to the fishpond—"

Fleet of foot, the councilor's wife stood up and was already hurrying across the terrace, as she said: "I hope my guests have finished their tea—You may perhaps be interested in taking this opportunity to view the park—" Her elegantly shaped legs ran nimbly amid the pleats of her skirt.—Fräulein Franziska came on smiling, with Doctor Zäuberlin and Andreas behind her.

Between the bushes they could see the black expanse of fishpond, the willows gloomily reflected in its brackish water. In the middle of the fishpond Niels was rowing in a small blue skiff. He laughed and waved to the group on shore. "Hallo! hallo!" he called and tossed back his head.

The councilor's wife had pulled out a lace handkerchief and waved as if to send a last goodbye to someone sailing away on a transatlantic steamer. "Hallo! hallo!" called the youth in the boat and his whole face laughed. "That's Franziska for sure! Good afternoon, Franziska old girl! Shall I come and carry you off in my boat?!"—And he rowed straight to her, was at the shore in a couple of strokes. Fräulein Franziska laughed darkly at him.

Andreas suddenly stroked the trees, ran his hands caressingly over their rough bark. He felt as if he were experiencing something for the first time, although he did not yet know what. "Trees," he said to himself, "grass—grass—" Never before had he felt such a sense of the earth, the ground beneath his feet, he felt as if he had to press his cheeks to the tree bark or his face to the yielding earth.

Fräulein Franziska, who may have heard his whispers, suddenly turned and looked at him.

Doctor Zäuberlin stood in the background, annoyed.

But the councilor's wife, her cheeks dimpled, waved her fluttering handkerchief to the boy in the boat.

2

Over supper in the Gothic dining room, things became

highly animated. The councilor's wife had appeared in full evening dress, her shape glistened with silver brocade and her plump white arms were bare. Her hair was also silvered with some sort of old-fashioned flower work and her eyelids, lips and cheeks had been discreetly made up.—The pomp of Fräulein Franziska, who sat across from her in stark white, was of a more gaudy, garish variety.

Doctor Zäuberlin was in uncannily high spirits, squeaked like a mouse, squawked like all the roosters in the world combined, and intermittently told jokes in a rasping Bohemian accent. He referred to the ladies as "My gentle creatures—my good creatures—" and, his bird's head suddenly bowed in respect, he filled their glasses with red wine. Consequently he looked like the leader of a coven of witches, who, amid much mischief and weird lore, is with volatile but earnest intensity brewing a love philter for beautiful ladies.

Niels, however, was wearing a blue suit with a small white turned down collar, which made him look half like a young naval officer and half like a student at an English boarding school. He flirted across the length of the table with Fräulein Franziska. He asked her about mutual friends in Berlin, laughed loudly at what she told him about them, and his voice sailed brightly through the room.—Then suddenly, still laughing at something Fräulein Franziska had impartially related, he held out his wine glass to Andreas: "Cheers, boy—" he called out and laughed even more heartily at Andreas's alarm.—The glass that Andreas held out to him trembled so much in his hand that the wine spattered over the tablecloth. Niels's laughter was contagious. Her head of heavy hair bent to one side, the councilor's wife laughed roguishly, with dimples in both cheeks. The laughter echoed strangely in the arched ceiling. Only Doctor Zäuberlin sat deadly serious, his mouth narrow as a knife, his face crisscrossed by malicious lines. His small, black eyes raced swiftly, hatefully, but imperceptibly over to Niels, who leaned back in his chair and laughed till he cried.

After the table was cleared, Andreas and the councilor's wife sat a bit apart over their coffee. With easy avidity, the lady drew out her young guest. "You must probably be surprised by much that you see here," she said and bowed her beautiful face deeply, "and my relations with Niels may not be entirely clear to you—" She had wrapped herself in a black silk cape and was shivering, although nestled deep within its folds. "My sole wish at the moment is to adopt him legally, so that our situation will stop being vulnerable to people's malicious misconstructions. The way the farmers talk," she said mysteriously, and shuddered within the folds of her cape, "Oh—the local farmers—"

Across the room Doctor Zäuberlin was conversing with Fräulein Franziska, as he waddled along on his small, bent, bandy sea legs. In addition, a pipe in his mouth, he spoke a North German dialect and made rude and folksy propositions to Fräulein Franziska who had to laugh coarsely at them.

"Doctor Zäuberlin is always reproaching me too," the councilor's wife said to Andreas and her mouth twitched touchingly, "he says I'd be too indulgent to the young man—once I've espoused his cause." She raised her white immaculate forehead which was as empty as her eyes and her voice. "I know so very little myself," she moaned and clasped her gemladen hands as if in prayer, "often I really don't know how I can help him, although I have lived through so awfully much all these years.—But you cannot judge how serious I am about this. Besides, I have always loved men in order to possess them. This time I love a man in order to assist him: there is quite a difference. I don't know whether you entirely understand me. But since you are his contemporary—" And she shook her head in perplexity.

Andreas, his face concealed behind the cigarette smoke,

only replied, "I do understand you—I do—I fully understand you—"

Suddenly Niels was standing beside them. "Having a nice chat?" he said and laughed at them. He stood close by, his hands in his trouser pockets and his fair hair over his forehead. His face was somewhat broad, but the eyes in that face were bright. "Am I disturbing you?" he asked and stood there with his legs apart.

The councilor's wife looked up at him and smiled painfully. "I do believe you should get your hair cut soon," she suddenly said. Then Andreas quickly turned his face away, as if to hide his tears.

But when Niels stood in the shadows, looming over the councilor's wife's head, she kissed his hand, which he calmly abandoned to her. She laid her face on his hand and covered it with kisses.

***

Later Andreas sat on the bed in his little room, rapt in thought. Outside, the murmur of the river blended with the indecipherable murmur of the night. The students were singing about the pursuit of happiness. "Gaudeamus" they were shouting out there in the woods.

Andreas thought, any minute now Doctor Zäuberlin will be riding up the chimney on a broomstick. He had better make a wide circuit around the madonna, who peers in wide-eyed charm through the branches of the apple trees or else his spells will be broken.

The magically deep charm of the place embraced Andreas. What nun may have lived and prayed in this little room?—He reflected devoutly on the young Mother of God who hung in pastel colors against the wallpaper. The sweet oval of her face was childlike and strangely veiled in silvery good humor. But it was filled with a touching sorrow that silently, gently lay in her

95

eyes, her eyebrows, so narrow and sensitive but rather tense.— Observant Andreas found that the woman's face bore a slight resemblance to the silent, helpless face of the councilor's wife, which was no longer young but mysteriously preserved its beauty intact.—She loved a man, not to possess him, but to assist him. "But basically he is almost incorrigible," she had said. And Andreas thought suddenly of the words a man had spoken to him in his dressing room—

He went next door to Fräulein Franziska, who was still up, fully dressed. Couldn't she sleep either, he asked.—Then they went arm in arm down the echoing stairs, for they had decided to take a walk in the park. The pathways stretched out black and arched. But Franziska had brought along the candle from her bedroom. Tightly pressed against one another, they walked in its wavering, flickering glimmer. Franziska's face grew to fantastic size in the unsteady light. At her side, Andreas whispered: "You look like the abbess of this cloister, the stern abbess." "Then you have been entrusted to my supervision, you young monk,—" the witty woman's coarse voice replied. "What a cowl you are wearing," the lad went on, "oh—what stiff folds in your habit—oh, what a shiny cross around your neck—" He ran on ahead and through the pointed arches could see a gateway in the dark park.

They stood outside the park by the stream whose gleam shimmered white in the darkness, and Fräulein Franziska picked a great bunch of sallow flowers.

In a room on the ground floor a light was still burning. They could hear voices behind the drawn white curtains, for the window itself was open.—Fräulein Franziska and Andreas walked arm in arm to this window, for they agreed in silence that these voices should be overheard.

The lifelessly resonant voice of the councilor's beautiful wife spoke at length and clamorously. "Why do you keep torturing me by saying you want to leave me, at the very time you know I want to bind you to me forever?!" she cried and grief lent her voice a quavering harshness, as when a mermaid has to lament and has no heart capable of lamentation. "But you know I cannot live without you!"—However, the boy's voice, brighter, crueller, glossier, replied: "Just why can't you live without me? Find someone else to experiment on. I'm fed up, I've had it up to here being a guinea pig for research into educational problem cases. If I were still your lover—" "You are still my lover," the woman's voice retorted with infinite tenderness, "you are still my only lover—" "Your interest in me is a teacher's for a schoolboy—." But she interrupted, "You get it all so wrong!" Then he, with the ruthlessness of his eighteen years: "There's no need for more talk: first thing tomorrow morning I'm clearing out! I'm going to Berlin, I feel more comfortable with Fräulein Franziska and that pretty boy who couldn't take his eyes off me all day, I feel a lot better off with him too—."

It was shocking to hear how the councilor's wife's voice took one last leap to quavering severity. "You will not!!" she cried and instantly corrected herself. "Neither God nor man could ever forgive you for doing such a thing—such ingratitude would be incredible!—Oh, you cannot be so common! After all I've done for you, to abandon me without a scruple! To cast me off after I took you out of the gutter! God knows how you would have been bought and sold without my intervention! You cannot be so common!" But his voice overtopped hers and, like an arrow aimed high, shot ramrod-straight and glittering to the sky. "If you only knew how much I despise your old-maid's way of talking! So you want me to pay up for all the favors you did me once—there's not a thing you can use to keep me here! I'm so sick of you and your fumbling—." And her voice again, subsiding once more and muffled in tears: "Such ingratitude—such dreadful vulgarity—."

Suddenly, as Andreas looked through the white curtains,

he saw both their faces: his face, overhung with fair hair, filled with passionate defiance, the eyes glowing hard, the mouth tightly shut. And her face, at a great distance from his, the immaculate brow bowed down, the eyes empty, drooping with tears.

Now he went to the door. Without once turning round, he said "Adieu!" and slammed the door behind him.—She straightened up at her little table, stretched both arms stiffly in the air, and with a bursting voice shrilled a brittle sound into space. The eyes in her face were glassy and dull. Her mouth was wrenched wide open in sorrow like that of a tragic mask.—She was a woman who had lost the ultimate in her life.

Driven by the scream, they both hurried into the garden, then into the park, back to the bushes—as if escaping.

When they finally stopped near the wall, all Andreas said quietly was, "Now he will come with us."

But Franziska did not respond. She was listening intently to the noises of the night.

* * *

The next morning, even before breakfast, Doctor Zäuberlin rapped at Andreas's door. He had on his white lab coat, which made him look quaintly like a trained monkey. "Forgive me for disturbing you," said his narrow mouth, "but my errand is of a painful nature."—Short, cunning and dead serious he stood there, and Andreas knew in advance what he had to say. All he thought was, "She couldn't have come up with a weirder emissary. She wants us to retain enchanted memories of her castle forever—" But the doctor was saying punctiliously:

"The mistress of the house bids me convey that the best thing for you and your friend would be to leave the convent. This is not meant as an affront, but only to signify that the councilor's wife has had a distressing experience, is now perfectly apathetic and wishes to see no one. The councilor's wife is often unwell," Zäuberlin said curtly and drooped his large nose, "she tends to periodic breakdowns, which gave her late husband much cause to grieve."

Andreas thought, in his chair: "The things that must have gone on in this convent in the past.—What a place to find him in—"

But aloud he said that he had seen the Doctor's message coming and expected it. "I send the councilor's wife my compliments as well as best wishes for her recovery. Naturally, in these circumstances, we shall leave the convent this morning."

But as Zäuberlin turned to go, Andreas asked, again politely: "Excuse me if I am being indelicate: may I ask whether you are presently engaged in seeking for gold?"

The doctor raised both hands in deprecation with a grotesque twitch: "Please," he said and made a face, "I am looking for the philosopher's stone."

3

The next afternoon, as Fräulein Franziska, Paulchen and Andreas were drinking tea in his large ex-dining room, there was a knock at the door, and little Henriette showed in Niels. "The gentleman wishes to speak to you," she said with a pallid curtsey in the doorway.

Outside the rain was coming down in torrents, water streamed down the windowpanes, but Niels was wearing no overcoat. His hair clung to his scalp and water ran over his face and hands. Paulchen, intimidated, remarked, "He looks like a soldier they pulled out of the river—I'm tellin' ya." Fearfully he pursed his delicate lips and no one was quite sure what he meant.

But Niels shook himself off like a dog. "Here I am," he said with a laugh. "I'm—I didn't have any more money for the train, so I ran all the way from Anhalt station."

Andreas only looked at him, the teacup frozen in his hand. He thought in confusion: here he is—now he's here—he's here now.—But he was glad that Niels seemed so much at a loss and in need of help. That way he could assist him and do him a good turn all at once. "You certainly are very wet," he said idiotically. A puddle was already forming around Niels, as the water kept flowing off his hair and clothes. Andreas brought out a dressing gown and slippers and carefully helped Niels put them on.

Niels changed his clothes without bothering about Fräulein Franziska's presence. He ran over to her in his short drenched shirt. "Well, how's it going, Franziska old girl?" he asked and suddenly kissed her hand.—Without laughing, she gave him a not unfriendly look, one almost devoid of severity. "How is Frau Gartner?" was all she asked, as she ate some cake. And Niels who looked twelve years old in his shirt replied: "Oh, she's all right—she's resting now—"

Later on, when Niels was muffled up in the long folds of the camel's hair dressing gown, he wanted to greet Fräulein Barbara, whom he had met here once before. Barbara was giving an intimate tea for ladies, but Niels was welcomed joyfully. "Niels is here! Niels is here!" they all shrieked and held out their hands to him through the sweetish cigarette smoke.

Barbara herself, vigorous and gentlemanly in a one-piece pajama suit, offered him a cigar which she pulled out of a wide pocket, merrily screwed in her monocle, and laughed with the whole of her crudely powdered child's face.—Fräulein Lisa was squatting on the ottoman with her legs tucked under her and her eyes blazed like drily flickering lanterns. And next to her, stretched out full length, was the anemic ballerina, languid and pale as a diseased odalisque. She half rose and smiled in bewilderment with her flaming cherry red mouth. "Who is it, Fatty dear?" she asked Barbara in a faint voice, but Barbara had already started to brew a kind of punch somewhere in the background. Niels bowed almost affectionately to the flaccid dancer, who was relaxing in a peach-colored pleated dress. "I'm it—Niels," he said and started toying with the funny little curls that fell sparsely over her brow.

Paulchen came in too, his shoulders nervously hunched. "Now we'll all be nice and cozy together," he said in his high voice. But the sidelong glance he cast at Niels was, nevertheless, somewhat distrustful. "And that's a fact," fat Barbara cried forthrightly from the background. She laughed winningly at Paulchen, but a certain anxiety dwelt in her eyes. She was still worried that her father might one day have her picked up by the juvenile correction police.—

Later Niels said hello to Widow Meyerstein in her sitting room. It was arranged that he would take his meals there for a while and find a room in the neighborhood. "You always blow such fresh air through our crowd!" said the widow and laughed till they feared for her well-being.

***

It had been decided that after the show at "The Mud-hole" they would go to the amusement park, the lot of them, to Luna Park—all together in one big group.

The meeting place was the entrance to the roller coaster, the roller coaster was their favorite. Not that they would have skipped the shoot-the-chutes, the diabolical shimmying staircase or the enormous Ferris wheel—that would have been unthinkable. They were attracted by anything that stopped and started and rotated and spelled noisy, flashy danger.

Fräulein Barbara drew up a radical program. "Next we'll go on the roller coaster three times," she said bloodthirstily, counting on her fingers. "Then the shoot-the-chutes twice, then the Ferris wheel once." And they also wanted to go in the funhouse with the distorting mirrors.—Paulchen, a lady's coat over his arm, was already trembling and chattering with exaggerated anxiety. "I won't live through it, I won't live through it!" he complained in a squeak.

Fräulein Franziska made impartial protestations. She frankly stated that she considered three times on the roller coaster too much. And did that allow any time for bar-hopping?—Anxiously debating these questions, they noisily went their way.

Weirdly stimulated, the pallid ballerina was dancing off to one side in a pink knit coat. Her rounded eyes gleamed in anticipation; she performed complicated exercises, nimbly bent over backwards so that her head touched the ground. The others were childishly delighted by it. Niels applauded and kept shouting "Bravo! bravo!" Fräulein Lisa smothered the supple girl in kisses. "You did that so prettily!" she whispered to her with burning eyes.

In their midst, Andreas, in a tight-waisted overcoat and no hat, became excited and expatiated verbosely on the fact that the roller coaster was far and away the finest, most wonderful ride of them all. He therefore insisted on riding the roller coaster three times.

Fat gentlemen passing by made fun of this motley crew of children. They would strike up a smirking flirtation with one of the young ladies or one of the young gentlemen.—Niels laughed so hard that he could be heard across the entire park. He took Fräulein Franziska by the arm and, tightly pressed together, they saw to the tickets.

They nearly filled a whole car, only two old ladies could find a seat in the same one.—Slowly the long line of cars rolled upwards—high up to the pinnacle of the scaffolding. Paulchen was already squeaking anxiously, well in advance, even before the ride—the rushing up and down part, the dizzying movement up and down—had actually begun. "I'm tellin' ya': this is the absolute end for all of us," Paulchen waffled and passionately twined himself round Andreas's arm.—Fräulein

Franziska was impassive and reckless. "Pooh, pooh," she mocked beneath her dark red trilby. Fräulein Lisa sat gracefully, submissive to her fate, and had put her arm around the little ballerina's shoulders.

Now they were at the top, below them Luna Park flashed, clamored, paraded. Loud clanging, spinning, shrieking came from beneath them.

The two unknown ladies had been whispering the whole way up. "Well, I never—every single one of them is wearing make-up"—but then the car came rushing downwards with all of them. It came to a clattering halt in the gulley so that one lost one's mind and clenched one's stomach at the same time.

They screamed all together: "Whee-ee-ee!," so that it shrilled over the amusement park. Fräulein Barbara's broad fedora was caught by the gale wind of the ride and fluttered darkly away. Paulchen's squeaking overtopped their voices, rattling away in deathly agony. Andreas tossed his head far back, totally out of breath. The ladies' screams, uttered in different pitches, blended with the resounding chorus. But over all else rose Niels's voice as, with closed eyes, he flung himself into Fräulein Franziska's arms.

That was the way they rode to Hell together.

4

Here is the big room in the boarding house: it is filled with cigarette smoke and amidst the cigarette smoke the gramophone is playing on the little table. The smoke and the tunes rise together to the ceiling, wild, rackety, crackly tunes and yearning, drawling ones. Bright gray smoke and the artful clacking of castanets. Sweet saxophone and fiddle music makes the air thick and heavy.

Four persons are sitting at a considerable distance from each other, dispersed about the big room—four persons in a smoke-filled boarding house room. Two of them leap up, for the gramophone is pining and enticing in a particularly crafty way; they meet in the middle of the room without a word and stalk rhythmically up and down.

Niels is dancing a tango with Fräulein Franziska, while close at hand Andreas and Paulchen watch them. When the music goes into a particularly fervent and passionate upswing, they too rise, embrace and dance together in their turn, far more bent over, more abandoned, less according to the rules than the first couple who, under the lady's stolid influence, are confined to what is proper. Paulchen and Andreas stray over the carpet in long, high strides, their heads sloping against one another—whereas Niels and Franziska draw themselves to the middle of the room with tiny circular steps, then suddenly stop, embrace more tightly, and with earnest eyes observe the intricate and impassioned play of their tiptoes.—That is what the tango demands.

As soon as the music stops, Paulchen and Andreas let go of one another, bow to one another with a swift smile, and then each one goes back to his place. But Niels keeps his arm around Fräulein Franziska's waist, and they sit side by side on the bed.—

They talked a bit, but their words came from a great distance, as if none of them could hear the others. "You have such a funny way of sitting," Fräulein Franziska said across to Andreas, "so bent over—." And she tried to laugh. And Paulchen's high voice could be heard from somewhere else: "Say what you like, last year's tangos had a lot more appeal—," while Niels suddenly asked for a cigarette.

They sat with heads lowered as if before a wind, and their glances shot past each other like their words. While Paulchen's lackluster eyes were dully fixed on Andreas, he looked over at Niels in total immobility. Fräulein Franziska did not take her black gaze from Andreas's face, as if she wanted to learn it through and through, and yet she did not flinch at the touch of

Niels, who was stroking her with both hands, leaning so close to her that she could breathe the fresh scent of his hair, as he said to her very clearly and brightly: "I've never liked you so much as today—."

Nor did she resist when he pressed her back on to the bed, calmly she let it happen. But as she sank back, her fixed gaze remained on Andreas.—And Niels, his eyes closed and his hair disheveled, whispered as he almost lay on her: "Wouldn't we like to turn out the light now—." And as it grew dark she could still see his mouth, half open as if to drink.

From the background Paulchen whispered with chattering teeth—for he had not the courage to shout—: "No, you mustn't do that—no, that's a dirty trick to play on Andreas— all night I've seen it coming—don't, don't—" he whimpered as if someone were hitting him, but the noises from the bed overwhelmed his little voice for they were louder.

Then, trembling all over, he ran to Andreas, who was sitting motionless, sunken in upon himself, as if he could never move again—no, never. In the deep darkness Paulchen kneeled down beside him, crouched there and kept caressing his feet as he spoke up to him, unable to see his face. "Fräulein Franziska's the one I blame," he said, cringing on his knees, "and in your bed at that—it's a betrayal by that Niels—." And since Andreas made no move, he lifted his face halfway to him: "Don't sit so still—I'm still here—."

And while Niels laughed and moaned over on the bed, this pale, distressed Pierrot face spoke mad, quiet words to Andreas: "I'm still here," the poor squeaking voice complained, "today I want to say—today you can see what you mean to that Niels, that bastard.—I didn't realize it the first time we met—I thought, we'll be nice and cozy together like good colleagues, and I thought you were appealing.—Anyway I don't get close to just anyone," he said and could find only silly words to express the perturbation of his heart which he could not understand or explain. "This is the first time I can think of—oh, if you would only be my friend."—Across the room the bed creaked and Andreas was overcome with terror as in a nightmare. But he realized that no dream could be so distressing and none so insane as this life in which we are alone.—And then the pale helpless one at his feet, who got no answer, let go of the chair back by which he had raised himself, sank back on to the floor and withdrew into himself.—The moans and broken chanting from the bed had subsided. Paulchen's poor little speech had dried up on the carpet like a trickle of water. "And anyway I don't get so close to just anyone—"

Andreas sat alone, unchanged, his hands dead in his lap and his head jutting forward as if his own face shocked him. Only the lips moved rapidly as if he were trying to pray. But he found no words, they were lost in the stillness of the room.

He stood up slowly and went slowly over to the bed. A very dim early morning light fell onto the sleepers from the window. Andreas stood beside them and looked at them. They lay full length beside one another, among the rumpled pillows, the blankets barely covering them. He was breathing deeply and a smile had settled around his mouth. But she lay as if stone dead, her brick red mouth strangely faded in the gray dawning and the lips pressed severely together. Her face was full of dark shadows, gray and blue, but the skin around her eyes, where her brows were darkly knit, had become smooth and the lids with their long lashes were shut in the most profound peace.— Down at the end of the bed, amid the blankets tossed together in confusion, her feet appeared, broad and touching in their black silk stockings. Next to them his feet were bright and bare.

Andreas knelt below these two bodies which lay united and indecent. And while Paulchen moaned quietly in his sleep in the corner, he pressed his face against the sheet on which Niels and Franziska had made love. On the coarse linen he found the words he had sought for earlier. "Our Father, Which art in heaven—"

Niels stirred in his sleep. He drew up his knees, adjusted his head in the pillows, but Fräulein Franziska's feet remained serene. Andreas prayed, his brow on the bed: "And forgive us our trespasses, as we forgive those who trespass against us."

* * *

He stood at the window and gradually the sky grew lighter. The great night was coming to an end, the darkness was paling, graying by degrees, the pink and yellow shadows were already climbing over the houses in a matutinal manner. A cool wind was blowing assertively down the street. Water spiraled in ice-cold, bright, thin waves under the drafts blown by the wee hours of the morning. Milkmaids and baker's boys were already trudging somewhere or other.

Then Niels straightened out in bed, looked around, put a hand on the forehead where his hair hung so blondly, as if a thought had crossed his mind—and stood next to Andreas. He opened the window wide and leaned his face into the fresh air. He was not fully dressed, for he wore only his blue trousers and an open shirt and was barefoot. He inhaled and laughed at the morning.

He was the young sailor who strides the deck of a morning when the sea awakes and swabs the planks with steaming water. He was the goatherd who drives his flock to the mountains of a morning, when the fields are still white, still frozen in the mist before sunrise. He was the apache, who after an adventure-filled night, steps out of the low dive of a morning—barefoot of a morning, and wearing blue trousers and an open shirt extends his face to the cold.

He turned his face to Andreas, and, his eyes suddenly downcast but a laugh still on his lips, he said quickly, quietly, but very brightly: "You aren't still mad at me, Andreas?"—But Andreas made no reply.

There was a loud knock, and a tall shape in a man's overcoat stood on the threshold. It was Fräulein Barbara, and she asked in an anxiously muffled voice whether Paulchen was there. It seemed she wanted to say goodbye to him, yes, she was leaving early today, she was expecting her father to send the juvenile correction police after her. "Is Paulchen here?" she asked again, suddenly more loudly and violently.

Paulchen was still asleep, crouching gracefully against the chair where Andreas had sat. Fräulein Barbara went over to him, fat and mournful she stood beside him. "Paulchen dear," she said, "goodbye—"

But he was asleep and did not hear her.

Franziska straightened out among the pillows. Her lank hair hung limply around her earnest face. "Good morning," she said into the room.

Fräulein Barbara addressed her little farewell speech to Paulchen, who was asleep and did not respond. "I really don't know when we'll meet again," she remarked bitterly, "but whenever, God willing, everything will be all right—" Awkwardly, impeded by the big overcoat, she leaned over him and cautiously touched his light wavy hair with her fingertips. "Adieu, Paulchen, dear!" she said again and her face was deeply shadowed by the big fedora.

Franziska had lain back in bed again and closed her eyes. But Niels and Andreas stood beside one another at the window. Niels had put his arm around Andreas's shoulders. "You mustn't be offended by me," he said, almost worried, "you mustn't think I want to hurt you—" And he blushed like a little boy who has said something too serious and is then ashamed of it.

The clear light of earliest morning fell upon them all.

*

A few days later Niels suddenly fell ill, unexpectedly ill, abruptly and feverishly, as is the case only with children. He lay in bed in a fever, his eyes glowing unnaturally, and drank lemon water in greedy gulps, half sitting up in the bed. Then he had to laugh, for it was so sour, and twisted his mouth and lay back laughing in the rumpled bed, to recline in silence and stare at the ceiling astonished at the thought that he was in such a bad way or toss and turn as he cleared his throat with a loud rattle.—But Andreas sat beside him and comforted him both with silence and with speech.

"Calm down," he said and soothed the hot hand with his own, lighter one, "keep still for a while—all you have to do is think of something secret, something loving and consoling—it may even be something funny and rude—and then you'll be able to shut your eyes right away.

"Of course you are not Niels and I am not Andreas. You are a fourteen-year-old peasant boy, seriously ill, but living on a little farm far below the village and without any special chores. You have been feeling bad for a long time now—naturally, father and mother are off in the fields with their work—you've got a sore throat and a terrible burning in your ears—but suddenly the old doctor comes in, looking white and wizard-like in his furcoat—he has ridden over, high on his horse. The old gentleman stares quizzically behind the lenses of his spectacles, and says, 'There, there, my little friend—what sort of game is this then?' Then he puts his big, cool ear on your hot chest and his clever old mouth to your hot feet—he is fluttering blackly like an owl in the darkness of the farm room—"

By this time Niels had closed his eyes, but Andreas went on with his story. "I thought you were getting on rather badly," he said and smiled at the face that lay, quite unconscious of him, with closed eyes, before him on the pillow in semi-darkness, "then too you are the young roadmender who was hit by my horse's hooves—oh, how the fever of that bruise must burn. But I am the black-clad prince who is holding strict audience beneath the half-defoliated trees in the autumn garden, although everything is covered with frost. The attendants bring forth the one who startled their lord's steed. But the prince—the only impassive one among the freezing pages— gently raises his hand and commands, 'Give this youth gold and silken garments—I have hurt him—this youth shall be as my brother, as my son, as my beloved shall he dwell in the castle—for I have hurt him—' And the pages, slender and trembling, take you into their midst, lead you unto the castle— while the prince, now suddenly alone, stands beneath the trees—

"Oh," said Andreas, "I shall tell you such a lot of things, all that I know. I know a good deal about us. I almost believe, dear Niels, that I know all about us. We are two children who have run into the woods and cannot find one another on the other side. One child has a head filled with plenty of thoughts and plenty of doubts—but the other one has such fair hair. How mysterious, how filled with noise, temptation and dismay is the night. No moon can be seen amid the black clouds today. Even the stars have lost their serenity and dart like will-o'-the-wisps as if the wind were tossing them to and fro. Isolated lights glimmer, probably from nearby inns. Dogs bark inhumanly, laughing their coarse secrets from afar. The frogs croak so loudly. I call your name, which is Ugolino. 'Ugolino!' I shout into space. Perhaps you call my name too somewhere. I can hear your cooing voice in the distance. My name is Kaspar.—But our names do not find one another, the wind plays catch with their syllables, tosses them back and forth, they meet one another—oh, they pass one another in the black air. Kaspar cannot see you, Ugolino, you are alien, lost, evanescent amid the bushes—sometimes you stand in one place, suddenly you're as calm as a tree, but he doesn't recognize you for the second time—your treelike calm is so different from your restlessness—and he runs past you again. But still you are his fixed point and if it weren't for you he would have been lost a long time.—Ugolino, I will tell you everything. You shouldn't hear it, but you do have your eyes shut, so you won't understand it all. The nights were stormy and unquiet, I will tell you everything that I went through during them—"

It was quite as if the youth in the bed had fallen asleep. He breathed so evenly and his face was still. The storyteller's voice moved so lightly over him that it could not wake him. "You are greater than I, for you are more innocent than I," the voice said to the sleeping face. "Therefore you are also holier than I. Now I know that a breathing mouth is more in the sight of the Lord than a speaking mouth. And that a pious man is more than a knowing man. And that a loving body is more than a wise head. And that a dancer is more in the eyes of the Lord than a writer or a painter. And that you are great.

"That, Ugolino, is my secret, my fairy tale, my sweet song—that is the fairy tale of my youth and my strife-torn times: we must be innocent, not intelligent. We must be pious, not proud. We must be loving, not questioning. The world is to be beheld, not comprehended. And only the body binds us to God—the body and soul that dwells in it—never the reasoning spirit. That is my song, I have heeded it by day, I have lived it through by night. I know no better one, I have no need of any other. I do not know whether I can forge it into a picture, but when the last hour comes, I can say to you: thank you for being here now—I have seen so much. Thanks, I can reply to you, thanks, my dear dark hour, for not forgetting me. I was mindful of you the whole time. The tenderness that I always had for you purified all my actions. But the body that you gave me, my physical being that you uncovered and bewitched, has bound me to the earth in joy and sorrow, for with this, my body, I have loved all things and most of all the beloved bodies of other beloved men. That is why I walk through all the streets out of curiosity and lust, the streets which open up to me—and that is why lust and curiosity were pious. My beloved hour: I have loved life as you commanded—it was a boisterous life—"

The voice speaking to the sleeping face broke off. Andreas fell silent and hearkened only to the deep breathing of the friend beside him. Meanwhile it had grown almost pitch dark.

But in the darkness the voice soon began to speak again, its words ran like water over the other's resting body. "How odd it has been," the voice told the body, "how odd, until I found you. What erring paths I had to walk. How difficult, how torturous it was. But a voice once promised me that I should find enlightenment and understanding. Have I found it now? Have I already understood?—But my heart dares not answer me—" And the voice told him the short and confused story of his life, how things had been until that hour.

There had been his father, clever and unpretentious, a father who wanted to help and could not. The father had had a son, both ambitious and jaded, who had grown up in times of perplexity. The voice told the friend of this father's friend, the stern and serene representative of his father's generation, whom the son hated, for this man had been able to do everything that he yearned, with futilely intense effort, to win by struggle. Oh childish, woeful mistaking: to try to bring to life a work of art out of the abstract needs of youth. An unfinished picture, cold and brightly colored, stood in the next room.

As the careful painter paints his pictures, so this voice amply and chastely arranged things which had hitherto been inextricably mixed and displayed them in a round, golden frame against a golden background. He himself stood in the very center, of course, but still he was delineated in the fuzziest manner, indeed, his outlines were not at all to be discerned. His father stood behind him, festively wearing a frockcoat as at that important birthday party and next to him stood Frank Bischof, whose narrow grizzled head and experienced eyes looked far beyond him. Distant relations whose blood flowed in his veins were smaller and remotely suggested. Either little in particular was known about them or Andreas at least had never troubled to inquire into their now yellowing fates. But they were well portrayed in this picture. Queer aunts with puffed sleeves and long skirts, though many possessed his own hooded gaze. Grandfathers, absurdly diminutive, were visible in the more distant background, with earnest eyes and imposing brows. And almost at the vanishing point, gently dissolved in the melting blue were the delicate Biedermeier lines of the ladies those grandfathers had loved, beckoning from a distance with their rose red shawls and bonnets, and perhaps they themselves had something more to say.—Next to Andreas, like two angels, stood the women who had so greatly assisted his frailty. One in dubious humility who, even though he might weep in her presence, nevertheless demanded that he find "the way out" and the other one more boisterous, more garish, more full of contradictions, but still similar in so many ways to the first—equally severe, equally gentle. Both also had the same black eyes and the tightly shut mouth, although the eyes of the latter squinted in such a sinister way, and those of the former were so shimmering and clear, although the mouth of the latter seemed so cruelly smeared red, and that of the former was still untouched.—Then the children were in place before him, the little ones. Marie Thérèse, sweet and roguish, put on airs, protected and guarded from the unknown. Peterchen, pert and merry, stared straight at things which he had not yet conquered and which impatiently awaited the battle in a cheerful state of readiness. Somewhat to one side, Henriette was gnawing on her lip in premature knowledge, a more sinister little fate already sketched out, already shadowed, which she had a foreboding in her confused soul would grow to be big some day.—Along the border and at the sides the shapes crowded in ever more motley a hodge-podge. There was Widow Meyerstein's cruel beefsteak face that grew torpid only at night in her bedroom, Doctor Zäuberlin's droll wizard's visage shoved in between, Barbara's hearty child's laugh rang out somewhere, and Paulchen's colorless Pierrot countenance, silly and aggrieved, crept along the curve of the frame. And over there—wasn't that the little daughter of the cab driver couple, lusting for adventure, who pathetically needed her best hat when she went out? Human faces—human faces—the councilor's wife's Grecian profile and her wonderful hair suddenly emerged, painted in by the voice. Fräulein Barbara's humiliated foster father—the stark grandmother with the blue cheeks—the voice said: "That was what it was like until today. Who knows what it will be like in the future?"

But then it obliterated everything, behaved as if nothing had happened, and gathered all its tenderness into a single question whose sweet and profound absurdity it realized even as it spoke it. Andreas bent deeply over the sleeper, so that his mouth almost touched him. "But you—are you willing to stay with me?" he asked—but the face only breathed and did not answer.

So Andreas straightened up again and sat as before in the dark on the chair beside the bed. Why had he asked that?—He had to smile. Yet he knew so well that it was not his lot or his fate ever to possess another. Why should this person stay with him?—But he did not know that the smile on his face twitched as if it were weeping.

Then he came up with one last disguise for himself and the other, the deepest game of all. "I am a poet," he said into the darkness, "and you are my dream."

*

6

"I'll see what I can do," said Andreas as he sat amid his make-up on the dressing table and toyed with a cigarette. "I've made far too many appeals to Doctor Dorfbaum already—"

Niels was pacing the dressing room with broad strides. "But if you need the money urgently—" said Andreas and stared at the cigarette smoke. Niels stopped and spoke doubtfully up at the ceiling. "I haven't the slightest idea where all the money goes," he said and angrily brushed the hair out of his eyes. "It's just as if it fell out of my pocket—" And he stamped his feet.

But Andreas was smiling again over his red and blue eyebrow pencils. "I shall see what I can do," he repeated, as he underlined his brows with a stick of charcoal.—Niels yanked him from behind by his hair. "Yes," was all he said. But Andreas shuddered at the touch and the sound of his voice. The bright quaver that shook it touched his heart and made it vibrate. "It's a matter of some three hundred marks," he said very mechanically. And the voice behind him repeated, "Yes—"

"It's time for Herr Magnus to make his entrance," another, more trenchant voice sounded behind them.—Frau Zeiserich, withered, skinny and glittering in her finery, stood at the door. "I hope I'm not disturbing the gentlemen—" she said sarcastically.—Andreas walked past her in silence and out the door. "Goodbye," she called out behind him and he involuntarily inhaled her cheap, overpowering perfume.—She remained behind in the dressing room.

On stage the master of ceremonies was making a comic introduction: "I have the pleasure and the satisfaction of presenting to this fun-loving audience a very charming young man from a good family, who will be glad to do his best and offer you some spicy bagatelles—"

Standing between the curtains, Andreas thought: "Three hundred marks—last week I borrowed five hundred for him—" But all his doubts were in vain when he felt that voice ring in his ears again.—He made his entrance and stood there, almost unaware of the presence of those wine-bibbers and steak-eaters who confronted him. He did not feel the lorgnettes of intrigued ladies directed at him or hear the fat grunts of the gentlemen. "He's a nice cleancut sort," said one and pointed a thick puckered index finger at the sailor with the made-up face. He recited the words of his poem, which he no longer understood. The one about the male hustler and the Day of Judgment having had no success, he now had another in his repertory. "If only I wasn't from a respectable family—You know how it is—," he said and put one hand on his hip.—But his friend's voice blew through his heart like wind through a harp. The audience of "The Mud-hole" passed expert judgment on his figure. "He's got good legs," said one connoisseur very loudly, "but I don't care much for the mouth—" "My father's high up in the government—oh dear," the youth exclaimed in depressed tones, "as you can well imagine, I am a real disgrace—sure am—" For a while he went on about what he might have become had he not been born in such inauspicious and middle-class circumstances. "Well, it doesn't look to me like anybody's forcing him to do it," opined a fat red madam in her box and giggled into her champagne glass.—Then the sinister dark apache woman came on stage, the one who earlier had sung about the lame dog and the bearded virgin—and the shady sailor—son of someone high up in the government—conducted a wild dialogue with the tart from the docks, that degenerated into screaming, frenzied slaps and the orgiastic trampling dance. "Those low-lifes got temperament," the fat gentlemen murmured to each another. And the red lady of the champagne avidly commented to her escort: "Look at his body now—he's a real refined one—" But the man, totally carried away, only sighed: "Her bust—just look, her arms and shoulders—," which understandably annoyed the lady.

Andreas walked back through the dark corridor to his dressing room. Paulchen was sitting on a trunk, dangling one lilac silk leg, and called out something as Andreas passed him. "Was it good?" he asked and smiled at him. But Andreas paid no attention to him and had already turned the corner that led to his dressing room.—Then the smile froze on Paulchen's face and he sat there with his frozen smile, a mournful doll.

Andreas stood at the door to his dressing room, which was ajar. He could hear voices inside. Alma Zeiserich's sharp female voice was audible: "Of course I realize you have to be careful about me—your dainty gentleman friend might get jealous—" and as she was still bleating out her laughter, the bright voice replied, "You referring to Andreas? Nah, I'm not married to the kid yet—" Then Alma lowered her voice to an appropriate delicacy. "Well if you aren't married to him, maybe you might be to me—" and tittered again, tinny and fastidious at the same time. But as she tittered, Niels said quietly, "As a matter of fact I'll marry anybody who'll have me—"

Andreas pushed back the door. Niels stood laughing in the middle of the room and the Zeiserich woman in her iridescent dress was clinging to him, running her hands lustfully over his face and body. "I'm going away tomorrow for a few days," she whispered to him convulsively, "come with me, my love—." And Niels, who had noticed Andreas by this time, merely replied: "Yes—yes—I'll come with you—" and closed his eyes as if he did not care to see any more.—Then Andreas took hold of Frau Zeiserich's shoulders from behind and jerked her back so that she staggered against the wall with a crash. She shrieked: "Mon Dieu!" and clutched at her throbbing skull. "Aha, the deceived husband," she hissed and her eyes turned yellow as if they were visibly filling up with baneful poison. In mock emotion she raised her lanky arms: "Scene of domestic tragedy!" she chaffed, "the cuckold exacts an awful revenge for his disgrace—" But then Andreas clenched his fists and with a bursting voice she had never heard him use before cried, "Get out! Get out!!" She moved to the door, still holding her bump of pain, and disappeared with a smirk.

Niels was still standing in the same position in the middle of the room, his arms dangling and his eyes closed. With a rage that stunned and lacerated all his senses, Andreas shouted into his face. "There's absolutely no point in my talking to you," he railed in a rush and with bitter, tormented glibness, "you aren't worthy of words and besides you can't understand a single one. How could I ever persuade myself, I wonder, that you ever had the slightest interest in me on any level? You must know how deep my feelings have been for you—or rather: you never did know!"

Next door, through the thin wooden partition that was all that separated them, Fräulein Franziska sat and eavesdropped. She had two admirers with her—the dear friend of the red silk lady of the champagne, who had stolen away from her on some pretext, and an iron gray, threadbare man-of-the-world in a tuxedo, who had honored Franziska for years with his practiced homage. The dear friend was saying over and over again, "You really have the most wonderful figure," in quite a surprising tone of voice. But Fräulein Franziska paid no attention to him, as she eavesdropped with black squinting eyes on the vicious words spoken next door.

"That it should be that repulsive female, that worthless creature," said Andreas, "you were making me a laughing-stock with, that's what I can never forgive you! No one would have behaved to me that way, no one that I picked up at the Garden of Eden or off the street. You are a pit of selfishness and immorality. You have no heart—no understanding—."

But Niels's face maintained a deep, almost mournful placidity. "I knew it,"—he said quietly, "yes—I could see it coming—." And a slight transient, incomprehensible smile flitted briefly and sorrowfully around his beautiful mouth.—Andreas did not see that smile and shut his heart to the sound of the voice. In the face of this unintelligible silence his rage grew and his wretched anger blazed up like a straw fire. Niels's body seemed to him enchanted. He saw him in the second rate, easily depraved elegance of a gabardine suit which he, Andreas, had had to pay for. That was where Alma Zeiserich's unattractive hands had enjoyed their vulgar, lustful game, that was where they had run along his whole body.—And Andreas screamed, his arm suddenly pointed to the door: "Get out! Go on, get out! Go to her, run to her bed! I can't look at you any more, I will not see you ever again—never, not at any price. Run to her bed—run to her bed!" he commanded again and again and threw himself on the chair before the dressing table.—Slowly and seriously, Niels left the dressing room. His bright eyes had turned almost black.

When Fräulein Franziska in the stiff feather trimmings of her evening gown walked in on Andreas a little later, he was still sitting, a sailor with a painted face, strangely rigid, bent over his make-up. Fräulein Franziska touched him gently and said, "So you're not getting dressed?"—Andreas turned his empty eyes, circled with red and violet pencil marks, up at her: "I still have to visit Dr. Dorfbaum," he said flatly and suddenly smiled, "I need three hundred marks—."

Outside Paulchen was dancing "The Bird's Evening Prayer" for the second time, an encore for the pleased audience. He glided in subsidence to the ground, rose up again, stretched, extended himself to the fullest in his ecstasy, transported by the movement that raised his outstretched arms, lifted himself on tiptoe, moving up and down, trembling, vibrating as if he wanted to soar into space, ascending to break loose in the void—his head bent a little to one side, that light, empty head, the mouth half open, the black painted eyes dissolved in intoxication.

The next morning Andreas awoke beneath little Henriette's keen gaze. She stood menacingly before him with the breakfast tray and though he was half asleep, she said: "Last night Herr Niels instructed me to tell you that he has gone on a trip. He's not coming back in the foreseeable future."— Andreas only asked quietly from his pillows: "Did he say where he was going?"—And his face was as pale as the sheets on the bed. "No," said Henriette and set the breakfast tray on the chair. Then Andreas turned his face back to the wall.

Outside Widow Meyerstein could be heard laughing to shake the rafters. Henriette poured tea out of the cheap teapot. But in the meantime she never took her eyes off Andreas, and so the tea ran, not into the cup, but over the chair and dripped down onto the carpet.

7

Around this time Andreas began to work again. He sat in the big boarding house room that had once been a dining room with a sketch pad on his lap and drew. Fräulein Franziska had taken a seat on the bed—her favorite sitting place—so that the boy at the window had discourteously to turn his back on her. Still neither of them paid that any heed.

While he drew lines and shadows, his head bent to one side, she spoke coarsely and slowly behind his back. She had propped her face on both hands and the black eyes stared hard at the banal pattern in the carpet. Her feet stood wide apart on the floor.—Why did she talk so much today? As a rule she went around squinting and observing.—Fräulein Franziska was telling the story of her life.

"It really is strange," she said choosing her words, her eyes on the pattern in the carpet; and she was instantly surprised that it was all coming out so muddled. "It's awfully funny to think that I actually have no country."

The boy at the window sketched lines and it was not easy to

120

tell if he was listening. Fräulein Franziska related: "My father was Russian and my mother was Spanish, a clever combination. I've inherited my mother's hair and color of eyes, but my figure and movements are reminiscent of my late father. When I was born, my parents were living in Vienna where my father had a business. For business reasons and I don't know what, somehow he had become a naturalized Austrian. My late father was an Austrian subject. We lived in Vienna until 1912, when we moved to Paris. At the time I was a child of eleven. I must have been a very odd little girl," said Fräulein Franziska and suddenly digressed into a smile. "I was always very dark and swarthy and Mama says that when I could barely read and write I was dragging the thick, dusty German classics out of our bookcase to pore over them—Goethe and Hebbel and Grillparzer—" And Fräulein Franziska laughed a hearty, ugly laugh, as if such things were quite unusual. Then she went on: "It was lovely in Paris. We lived in a house in a nice district and my Spanish mother was very active. My father was often away on business and we gave a party almost every night. On the whole my mother was very annoyed that I wasn't dainty enough. My head in particular was a mess and I always looked silly in a white silk blouse, what with my black horse's mane standing on end and my angry eyes. At the time my one little brother was still alive, and I loved him like nothing on this earth. His name was Alexander, after my father. We had decided that we wanted to be writers: he would make up the stories and I would elaborate them. We were able to create the most beautiful plays and novels together. I couldn't do it on my own.—When we had lived in Paris for two years, which are like a dream to me now, the war broke out. I was thirteen at the time, and I hadn't a clue why it had happened. I was only concerned with Hebbel and Grillparzer and my beloved Alexander. The first week after war was declared we stayed in our house in fear and trembling. We were strictly forbidden to go out in the street, without my understanding why, and nobody came to visit us. My beautiful mother wept all day long, and my poor father kept pacing the floor. I can still remember him saying, a bloody sword will soon appear in the heavens.—Meanwhile the fact that we were Austrians became common knowledge. As we all sat together in one room, we could hear the mob gathering in front of our window. I can still hear the street urchins shouting: "Il faut tuer les boches—il faut tuer les boches!!" My mother immediately fell into a fit and they started rattling the front door downstairs. Stones clicked and banged against the closed shutters. Every crash made my mother twitch and grow more violent. My father—even today I don't know what he had in mind—suddenly walked out on the little balcony and tried to talk to those people. "Nous ne sommes pas de boches!" he kept shouting and held up his arms to protect himself on the little balcony. But he kept getting the same stupid, enraged answer: "Il faut tuer les boches—il faut tuer les boches!" A stone hit him in the forehead. He staggered back into the room, blood streaming down, his eyes swimming in blood, we thought at first he had been blinded.

"From that moment, everything changed. That was all I noticed and all that was clear to me: everything was now changed. I was separated from my father and little Alexander and went with my mother into a camp for women. I never saw either my father or my brother again. Alexander died of some contagious disease, I was to find out much later, and soon father died too, the result of his terrible head wound.—Our grand house was taken away from us and everything we owned. I can't remember how long we had to stay in that camp. My beautiful mother became more still and silent, she almost stopped looking at me and finally I was frightened of her. One day we women were sent back to Vienna. We hadn't a penny to call our own. Mother and I had to work in a factory. Naturally Mother's health could hardly take it, but I was always pretty hardy. Otherwise we were treated almost as badly there as we had been in France, for they took us to be enemy Russians.—Obviously I could not be a writer under those circumstances, I didn't have that much fortitude, and the confusion within me and around me was much too great. But I don't really believe our era needs writers.—As you can well imagine, all this drove Mother completely insane and she was sent to a free clinic. I was very alone in the city and was put in a boarding house with strangers."

Fräulein Franziska narrated slowly and coarsely, her voice almost indifferent, the way one tells the plot of a sinister but conventional novel. "No one can blame me for finding factory work too idiotic," she said sulkily, "or for going with the gray bearded old baron who made advances to me. Because I had such lovely legs and black eyes, the old gentleman put me in a dancing school and later a cabaret. He was the first—." And she closed her eyes and stretched. "Where would I be now if I'd thrown myself in the water then, which I naturally considered doing every day?" she said, her arms outstretched, as she smiled up at the ceiling. "At first I kept dreaming about my father, his eyes filled with blood, and my sick mother and my beloved brother. At first I kept going for long walks and my mind was confused, I had the notion that I was marooned and totally at sea.—But later I learned to love the body—" And she fixed her gaze on the ceiling, rose and walked over to Andreas. With legs apart, she stood behind him as he sat over his sketch.

"I don't know whether it makes one a writer," she said and put a hand in his hair. "I don't know what the outcome will be—." Her voice stroked him even more intimately than her hand. "I do know, Andreas, that you have been through something similar. And you are alone too—." It was touching to hear how her coarse impartial voice was modulated to a most peculiar delicacy. "But that's the way it is with most people, if they were to tell you their stories," she said, "here in the boarding house—and everywhere—. Our youth began amid upheaval and insurrection. Where will it end?"—And this question, which neither of them had been able to master, which they so often forgot in another deep smile, took shape before them. Where would it end?

He turned his head to her, as she stood bent over the back of his chair. "Is it like this everywhere?" he asked her big mottled face, "in Meyerstein's boarding house and every: where—?" And she replied without flinching, though her hands held his head a little tighter, like an invalid's: "My little Andreas—I know you cannot love me—you do not love women—we will not tell one another lies, we will not make it easier for ourselves—but let me have your mouth." And before he had time to answer, she took his mouth with her red-smeared one.—

When she was sitting quietly on the edge of the bed once more, Andreas came over, sat down beside her and showed her his picture. They bent over it together, so that their heads nearly touched.

A tall, half-naked youth was kneeling in the middle, at play with two children. He was tossing a ball in the air—his arm was still extended in motion—and the children were laughing at it: a little girl and a little boy. "It's got to be colored in now," Andreas said and smiled at the charcoal sketch. "It's not much, I wanted to draw a likeness of the Good Lord with His eyes fixed in wisdom. This is only Marie Thérèse and Peterchen playing with Niels. I had a special fondness for that idea: my little sister playing with Niels. I have always dreamed about it. And of course Peterchen has to be in it too—."

But with her face still bent over the picture, Fräulein Franziska suddenly said, not intending to frighten but with distrustfully knit brows, as if airing a vague doubt: "Just now we were wondering what was to happen next.—What if the world simply goes under?" And she laughed gloomily over the sportive bodies that Andreas had drawn.

But he merely replied, not seeing the logic in her gloomily frivolous notion: "Bodies have souls: that is the secret—everything hinges on that, everything is related to that—"

And as he spoke, he heard Niels's voice asking: "And just what is a soul?"

FOUR

1

IT WAS no easy matter to draw information out of "Rosepetal." Dr. Dorfbaum and Andreas had even invited him to their little table at the "Garden of Eden," plied him with white bordeaux and flattered him in every conceivable way. Dr. Dorfbaum, fat, snobbish but not unamiable, put himself out in the most disinterested way, although the finding of Niels must have been irksome, not to say painful, for him. "That young man is enormously important to us!" he said, not entirely without severity, and drummed his fingers on the table.—Andreas was silent and anguished. "If you really know where he's gone," he said hastily and poured "Rosepetal" more wine, "then stop holding out on me—I absolutely have to see him—." A certain something audible in his voice made "Rosepetal" turn a trifle serious. "By the way I have to get money for my information," he suddenly said quite coolly. "I haven't paid for my new shoes yet—"

A former dancing partner called to him. "Oops—an old friend!" he rejoiced and flitted away. Andreas and the doctor stayed behind, silently. "We'll get it out of him," good old

Dorfbaum comforted, but Andreas stared wearily into the cigarette smoke.

When "Rosepetal" came dancing back, he began cruelly to tease again. "How come I'm supposed to reveal information about his hidey-hole?" he asked with a simper. "I'm jealous!" And he suddenly put his hand in front of his mouth and tilted his head. Once they gave him fifteen marks, whatever he knew came to the surface.—Neils had gone to Hamburg where he found employment in a small "Upper Bavarian"-style establishment, dancing his version of "country clogging" every night.

Andreas had to smile. "Thank you," he said and stroked "Rosepetal's" graceful but withered hand. It was wearily toying with the banknotes Dr. Dorfbaum had put into it. "Rosepetal's" motley aging face was bowed over the old greasy notes. Little wrinkles were scattered all over it, and there was something pendulous about the dyed brown sideburns.

A loud sound of weeping came from somewhere. It was Boris who was bent over his table sobbing, for the owner wanted to ban him from the club. The weeping was mixed with shrill screams from the bar on the opposite side. Leaning on the counter, one fellow with beautifully waved flaxen hair was singing:

> Wait, you too will come a cropper,
> Haarmann's coming after you,
> With his handy little chopper
> He'll make mincemeat of you too.

"Rosepetal," bowed in rapture over the fifteen marks, hummed along—it was a homely little folk tune.

Across the table Andreas and Dorfbaum made plans to go to Hamburg the next morning.

***

It was time to say goodbye to Meyerstein's boarding house.

Since financial affairs with the tenant Andreas Magnus had, in every case, been settled to her relative satisfaction, the widow herself was amiably disposed. She laughed cordially, said "Goodbye" in English, and squeezed his hand vigorously. She had even packed him bulky sandwiches, if only in newspaper, so that he would not be without refreshment on the train. "Recommend my boarding house to all the young people you meet out there," the widow said with an all-encompassing gesture, and her face was turgid with laughter.— Professor Sonn, who was breakfasting with the widow, walked over and stared unsympathetically through the lenses of his eyeglasses; then he relented, for he said, "So the bird's about to fly away?," a tinge of affability despite it all.— Andreas walked over to the grandmother, sitting starkly before her sewing table. She turned the big bluish expanse of her face to him and surveyed him with fixed attention. A large, blindingly white piece of linen, on which, however, she was not working, lay upon her lap in heavy folds. Beneath them her knobbly old woman's hands lay as if frozen. "Train travel," she said and shook her head sternly, "make sure you get home safe and sound."

In the dark room, Andreas bowed over Fräulein Anna's bast- and metal-work. "You are a hard worker," he said, but neither of them laughed. They held a brief, earnest conversation. "Yes," Anna replied, her broad face bent over her coarse but finely articulated hands, so begrimed and nimble. "What else is there for us to do, if not work hard? Hard work is the only salvation that I can see—the labor of the hands—labor—." "I'm going to look for my friend," said Andreas shyly—and looked at the many objects she had manufactured and that surrounded her, bowls, little baskets, jugs. "I have to be on my way now—." "Yes," Fräulein Anna retorted, "everyone hopes he is doing the right thing—." And then they took one another's hands.

Amid the disorder of her room Fräulein Franziska sat gloomily over her lute. Her rough hand with its gleaming nails strummed it. "Adieu," was all she said, and he kissed her hand for the first time. She felt his lips on her hand and said over his head: "Say hello to Niels—" They both shuddered, a shiver ran down their backs, anxiety overcame them for no clear reason. "When shall we meet again?" asked Andreas. And, over him, she said, "We don't know."—They kept their heads bowed as though in the face of a great wind.

At the house door, Henriette was waiting for him. "I still have to say goodbye to you," she declared and curtsied grimly. Andreas took her hard, tiny hand in his. "Be good," he said and looked at her ugly little face with its sparse hair combed back, "grow up—" And she earnestly nodded at his words. "I wish you the same," she said simply. She stood before him in a pink cotton frock. He felt her gaze, warning and questioning, but then she was gone.

Fräulein Lisa was next to step out of her room in a violet morning gown; she laughed meekly and touched him for five marks. "Life is hard," she said and closed her eyes for a second. Her pale girlish face with the rather too sharp chin was so weary that it looked as if all the daemons together could not help it any more.

But Paulchen walked out to the car in his yellow house-coat. "Goodbye," he said and anxiously pursed his lips. "I'll write you when I get a chance—"

Herr Dorfbaum's fat face was already protruding from the car window. "We should be there!" he said and nodded.—But Paulchen's dim eyes were filled with tears as he opened the car door. "I really will write you when I get a chance," he repeated, as the car was rattling down the street.

As the car drove away, he stood in his pajamas on the windy sidewalk for a long time and waved his light hand in the air. The movement was like a surprised bird flapping its wings in anxiety.

Then he slowly walked back up the steps.

2

The bar on the Reeperbahn was jolly and well-managed, but Niels was no longer to be found there. Buxom blondes in tight-fitting Bavarian peasant costumes were amusing the audience of gentlemen here, though one could also enjoy the lads in their short leather pants. The Upper Bavarians who noisily filled the smoky tavern seemed altogether to be of uncommonly gloomy disposition. There might be shouts of "Deanderl," "Bua" and "Hoihoteho!"—but it all sounded a bit artificial. Folkloric acts were performed on a platform of planks. Taking turns, three ladies sang a stately ballad chock-ful of horrors, an old man played the accordion, and a little girl frisked merrily in a little flowered skirt. Niels had danced here too.

In fact, it was the graceful girl who was able to provide information about Niels's stay. He had made friends with a gentleman, the child reported as she, for all her gracefulness, guzzled a number of stiff grogs, yes, with a tall, refined gentleman-friend. The girl named the city where they had both gone. The gentleman's name was Baron Pritzlewitz, if she was not mistaken.—Doctor Dorfbaum had to smile at that. Yes, yes, yes—it was a small world. For all that, he was rather glad that even on this peculiar expedition he would be in contact with upper-class circles.

Over the course of the night the drunken child showed the gentlemen the Sankt Pauli district. Slender and lewd, she ran ahead of them, always eager and curious about the sinister, explosive racket of this fantastical harbor district. The air here seemed heavy with noxious vapors. Equivocal representatives of all races and nations elbowed each other in the glaring lamplight or the semi-darkness.—Sailors went in and out wherever a sign read curtly and impartially in English "Public House," bawling in groups or threatening in isolation. At the Hippodrome uproarious women were exhibiting weary-legged horses with pride and their own blowsy beauty with cupidity. In the narrow street they moved single-file, leaning on the house walls, one had to squeeze past others and the worst names were shouted back at them.—But where the sidestreet became gloomier, the drunken little guide pointed her index finger at the dull red lights at the entrances of low dives. "This is only for gentlemen," she said and laughed, her eyes gleaming and her shoulders hunched. "Very exclusive—"

Under the red lamps and amid the reeking vapors of greed, Andreas walked slowly, his hands in the pockets of his overcoat, silent but as curious as the debauched child guide. With rachitic legs in cheap green silk stockings she skipped roguishly ahead, while Doctor Dorfbaum, fat and elegant in a long woollen overcoat, beads of sweat on his brow, stumbled in the rear.—Such was Andreas's guard of honor.

The whores crooked their fingers enticingly and called out, "Hey, sweeties! Want to give us a try? Three marks for love in the dark—" But the girl dancer, as indefatigable and restless as a will-o'-the-wisp, wanted to show them more, giggling and promising that the most mysterious was yet to come.

While the morning was turning gray, they were still on the move. Dorfbaum's troubled face was grayish white and drenched in sweat. He was so tired he could barely stand on his feet. Andreas had the disheveled hair and the red, strained eyes that travel and adventure always gave him. But when the inquisitive little girl in the short pleated skirt stood before one dive and promised with glittering eyes, "You've really got to see this—these are the morning hustlers," Andreas followed her. He leaned against the wall in his long, tight-waisted over-coat. His face was very pale in the morning light, but his mouth was as hot as if inflamed. "Yes, yes, the morning hustlers," he said smiling into space and suddenly closed his eyes.

Then Dorfbaum could not resist either and stumbled after him down into the dive.

* * *

The next morning they had to be on their way again. Who knows how long Niels had stayed in the city where, according to the girl's information, he had received temporary aristocratic patronage.

The two barely had time for two hours' sleep. They sat facing one another with lackluster eyes in a first-class carriage.

Flat and barren, the landscape slipped by. The smoke from the engine fell heavily onto the black fields and slowly rose again. It looked as if the fields were on fire.

The men in the compartment spoke only a little. They leaned their heads against the upholstery and preferred to shut their eyes. Sometimes Doctor Dorfbaum would suddenly start talking in irritation and annoyance. "When I chance to picture your future," he suddenly said and his face was distorted, "I am faced with the worst, indeed the most hopeless prospects. I am certainly unable to conceive a positive solution to it all. You need a friend," he declared and held up a hand in exasperation, "who will stand by you and really help you!"

Without looking at him, Andreas only replied, a cigarette between his fingers, "I don't need anyone else."

"I might perhaps be your Mr. Right, I might perhaps be the one you could trust in," the Doctor complained. "But you won't have me." His upraised hand sank, his eyes filled with perplexity and need once more. "Yet you travel about in search of that young man who can give you nothing, you organize a wild-goose chase in pursuit of him, and after all he doesn't want to have anything to do with you, even if you find him. I really believe you are deranged!" he said suddenly and was immediately terrified by his simple discovery.

Andreas, watching the bleak landscape glide by, replied: "I never forced you to come with me—" His tongue was long weary of the torment of these fruitless, apparently hopeless arguments.

Dorfbaum was already seeing reason and becoming submissive. "No, no, certainly not," he said flatly, "I'm very glad we can be together—you might have chosen Paulchen or someone else as your traveling companion—you really are so discriminating—"

And so they traveled without agreeing about the third party who was being sought by the passion of one of them.

* * *

On the city on the Rhine that had been named to them, Niels was, of course, no longer to be found. Naturally they called on Baron von Pritzlewitz at his home, which was cramped and overstuffed and somehow reminiscent of Dorfbaum's in Berlin. The Baron was very tall, but with a dessicated face. His mouth was ugly and sunken in, and his eyes were lackluster despite a square monocle in a black frame. "No, I have nothing more to do with that young man," he said and smiled arrogantly, "I honestly do not know where he has got to. Dear me, a youth like that is passed from hand to hand—" The Baron's clothes were as wrinkled as his ugly face—a gray suit and patent leather shoes: elegant but musty. "Of course, of course," said Doctor Dorfbaum somewhat too quickly, "you are absolutely right—"

Andreas, who sat uncomfortably between them, thought it rather comic that both gentlemen should be wearing monocles, one round, the other square. They bowed to one another a good deal and were very courtly in their replies.

Finally Von Pritzlewitz showed him his valuable little

antiques in ebony caskets, silver vessels and choice bronzes. "Yes," he said, "a civilized person needs such things—"

And when they said farewell, he declared once more as he held out his slender hand and smiled spitefully, "No, I do not in fact know the slightest thing about the young man. Incidentally, he turned out to be *charmant*," he added objectively.

* * *

In the hotel room Doctor Dorfbaum and Andreas said their goodbyes. Doctor Dorfbaum had to get back to Berlin.

"I wish you much luck in your quest," he said, but his smile was wan. "I wish you much luck in everything." He was standing with a big bouquet of red roses and looked like a grotesque bridegroom. "Don't think too badly of the time we spent together," he went on and his bright blue eyes were peculiarly fixed. And from his hotel chair Andreas said, as if something remarkable had suddenly become clear to him, "Yes—it's all over now—" and his eyes and those of the mournful gentleman filled with tears.

"If you run out of money, you know whom to turn to," Dorfbaum went on.—In the end he had bought the picture of Niels playing with Marie Thérèse from Andreas for a disproportionately high price, to prevent putting him in his debt too directly and baldly. "This way I have a picture of your darlings," he had said with rueful facetiousness.

"Yes," said Andreas, "thanks."

Fat and dismal, the Doctor walked slowly to the door. "There's still so much that needs to be said—but my train's about to leave," he said and waved for the last time as he left the room.

Sitting bolt upright at his table, Andreas once again read a card that had been sent to him there. "My dearest Andreas! I think about you almost every day. I don't know what I'm doing any more. Maybe I'll see you soon. Your Paulchen."

Andreas let the card drop. He thought he might be able to weep now, but the need that strangled his heart was of a kind that could not be dissolved in tears.

Paulchen's handwriting was so anguished a scrawl.—

3

Around this time Andreas learned to read again.

As when he lived in his father's house, the books lay around him in little piles or were arranged in rows on tables and shelves or strewn over all the chairs and even the bed, opened or with bookmarks in them. Scandinavian books and German ones and French and English books. He read almost the whole day through and into the evening, stretched out in bed with the night table lamp burning beside him. The interweaving clouds of cigarette smoke filled the relatively comfortable hotel room. At intervals the great bell of the cathedral that was located almost directly across from his hotel clanged and sang.

Then how the little room filled with forms. Songs struck up in all the corners, tunes ponderous and light came from above and below. Great laments grew loud, the eternal sorrow of all creatures arose and sang and a sublime radiance, the hope of peace and enlightenment, shone.—Andreas Magnus sat amid all this, his head propped on both hands and read and read.

One man had seen the forests and how God laughed and clamored in them. He had seen the trees wherein God, unruffled and mighty, manifested Himself. He had seen women and girls, whom God had made His sport and His miracle. He proceeded to tell of the forests, the trees and the women. His name was Knut Hamsun and he dwelt in the far north. In his hotel room Andreas Magnus read his stories dealing with God Who exercised His great guile throughout a personified nature. The forests rustled, the trees stood firm in the wind, the women tormented themselves and others with enigmatic charm.—In his hotel room the dreamer propped his head on his hands and looked on them.

Another man had lived elsewhere, in the land of America— he was dead now and purified—he had known everything about the body and had sung "The Body Electric," had told of it, laughed at it, wept over it in childishly, powerfully, chaotically ecstatic hymns in prose. He was more full of life than any of them, his proud body bound him most intimately to this world and its mysterious splendor. And yet he too, "pensive and faltering," put down these words: "The Dead." "For living are the Dead," sang the dithyrambic singer of the body and its strength, and added in pensive parenthesis: "(Haply the only living, only real, And I the apparition, I spectre.)"—Andreas sat bent over Walt Whitman's songs. He did indeed know everything about the body—he had heeded and aimed at nothing else, he said: "I see the body, I look on it alone, That house once full of passion and beauty, all else I notice not,—That wondrous house—that delicate, fair house— That immortal house more than all the rows of dwellings ever built! Or white-domed capitol with majestic figures sur- mounted, or all the old high-spired cathedrals, That little house alone more than them all—poor, desperate house!— Unclaimed, avoided house—take one breath from my tremu- lous lips, Take one tear dropt aside as I go for thought of you—" That was how he had spoken in America of the dead body of a streetwalker he had found in the morgue. And many years later, a certain Andreas Magnus bent his face to this song and understood it.

Over the body which Walt Whitman had dared to celebrate with orgiastic and childish effusions, another man, more arrogant, more solitary, more alienated, in Germany had sung songs which were lissome and gracefully noble as the sweet body to which they paid astringent homage. If the former had let his body flow like a holy cataract, the latter had wrought the most delicate and severe image from it. Where the former had opened his arms to a democratically erotic camaraderie, for the sake of the beloved love of men, the latter had set himself and an aristocratically élite circle above and beyond the masses.—Andreas Magnus pronounced Stefan George's most wonderful love songs, which collected great joy and great sorrow for the body and distilled them into the most pliant form, in his smoke-filled little room. Then he understood fully the profound connection that existed between the hieratic, exclusive devotee of "Maximin" and the press agent for "Love the Electric" and he could love them both.

He walked to the window and looked out at the spire of the cathedral until he grew dizzy. Before the cathedral was a circular plaza, teeming darkly with people. Tiny tramcars traversed it ringing their bells. How absurdly this bird's eye view diminished everything!—Soldiers marched by. A miniature noise, a ridiculous jangle came fluttering upwards.—But the cathedral sang and boomed over the plaza.

Andreas walked back into the room. He stood for a while before the mirror, where his face looked back at him amid semi-darkness and the gray smoke—a little boy's face, already worn out with living and traveling. He suddenly thought: there are soldiers marching outside, each one with his own body. Each one lifts his legs and his feet hurt. Each one has hair and eyes and mouth. Each one bears the enigma of sexuality. In the evening each one shares an angry altercation or a joyous sense of fellowship with his bride. Or an intimate, discreetly concealed friendship with a comrade.—And there are so many women as well, many women, each with her own body, fat women, thin women, women of every size. A forest of women, a forest of women's bodies and the fates of those bodies.—And Andreas suddenly said to his face: "What is to become of them now?"—And a shudder of fear, panic ran down his back and throughout his body, perhaps only because his voice suddenly grew loud and rang out a little more boldly in a room that had been so silent. But for the very first time he had not intended this question: "What is to become of them now?" to refer to his own generation.—It had developed into an anxiety about everyone, all these bodies and what God intended to do with them now. "What is to become of them? Where is all this leading?" he thought again more quietly and rubbed his hand over his brow.

Three faces stared out of the shadows at him ever more clearly, which seemed to him of all the writers the three most tested, the three most blest, and it was them he loved most.

He beheld the Scandinavian, though homeless, the teller of tales, at the age of eighteen. The handsome head was turned away from him, the dark eyes stared into the distance. The books he had later written all lay beside Andreas, who knew them almost by heart. The melodies of those books all had the same refrain. Their content was always: he who is too deeply associated with death will be homeless on earth. Therefore the homeless on earth loved the bodies of their beloved with a hopelessly ardent love: this is what the books related. All this the sorrow in the eyes of the boy's averted face had long understood.

Andreas loved him as his dear brother.

But another face appeared to him in the darkness. It resembled the skull of a degenerate faun with a straggling beard, a bald forehead and a drunken stammering mouth. At first Andreas supposed it would have the clouded eyes of a beggar but then he recognized the look of prayer in this ravaged face. Andreas believed he knew what those eyes had had to look upon before they assumed such drunken, Marian devotion. Only one who had gone through all the arcana of the body was ripe and pure enough for the other revelation. The polluted old man had borne witness to this in magical verbal images. His mouth had sung both mysteries, which were inextricably intertwined, only because he had been so ardently enmeshed in the first could he enter into the second so marvelously.

Young Andreas bowed to this poet as if he worshipped that face.

The third face that showed itself to him was also degenerate, puffy, tormented, dead tired as if having gone the way of the Cross. What had been the Passion of this life, begun in brilliance and artifice and which, it would seem, should have ended in mundane resplendent fame and arrogance?—The love of the body had been the Passion of this life. It was doomed, after the superficially buoyant mood of its triumphal youth, to stray even deeper in the labyrinth of love. The audacious contention of his daring youth as a dandy and an artist had been that life was to be a scintillating pleasure. He learned to grasp that life was sorrow, through love of the body. His Way of the Cross led him upwards from station to station, until he was summoned by death.

The legend of these lives deeply frightened Andreas.—

The first one's love had been the same hopelessly ardent devotion as his love for life, in which he felt himself an alien. The second one's love had been the dark, unfathomable passage through which he would enter the other love. The third one's love had been the Way of the Cross, which he had to travel to a knowledge of sorrow and a knowledge of death.

These were the poets Andreas most loved. These were the names to which he felt most intimately bound: Hermann Bang, Paul Verlaine and Oscar Wilde.

***

When he looked up, there were the roses that Dr. Dorfbaum had given him. They were already faded, blackening, and almost without aroma. A pair of photographs stood among the books. His father, Marie Thérèse, Frank Bischof

139

and Ursula looked at him as if they all wanted to know the same thing about him.

4

A young gentleman is outside, the maid announced and showed Paulchen into the room. Paulchen stood in the doorway with mouth anxiously pursed and did not sit when Andreas offered him a chair. He was wearing the ladylike pleated overcoat and the gray fedora. His shoes were long, pointed and bright yellow. He cleared his throat and seemed to be grievously embarrassed.

Andreas smiled encouragement at him and began the conversation. "I'm glad you're here," he said and asked whether he had an engagement there and was going to perform. But Paulchen shook his head. No, he didn't have an engagement. "I'm only here on business, yes, something to do with Meyerstein," he improvised on the spur of the moment and blushed fleetingly at the lie.

Then he sat down after all—coquettish as ever, his needlessly wide trousers hiked up to reveal his legs in their bright silk stockings as far up as the calf—and yet with such self-control as to be able to tell anecdotes. Yes, Widow Meyerstein had finally got engaged. To Professor Sonn, of course. But she had no intention of giving up the boarding house that bore her name. She wanted to be self-supporting and earn her own keep. Paulchen found that entirely reasonable—he was to convey greetings from Henriette, she was thinking of him. "That one's really smitten with you!" he suddenly shouted out loud and clapped Andreas on the shoulder like a gay blade. But then his hands immediately sank back into his lap—those lavishly beringed, yet weightless hands.—Fräulein Lisa was not doing so well. She was constantly out of money and would probably have to marry one of the dark, uncommunicative Theosophist gentlemen

140

soon. And Fräulein Anna was still working in her dark room with bast and metal.—But when Andreas asked him whether he had any fresh news of fat Fräulein Barbara, Paulchen only smiled anxiously at the tips of his shoes. "Yes, she's still in the reformatory," he said and shook his head in perplexity over it.

Paulchen had something to hand over from Fräulein Franziska, whom Andreas had, incidentally, not yet inquired after: a little present he would give him later on. "She's on the outs with the Zeiserich woman," he could report, "right now she's singing at an operetta theatre—yes, in a satirical revue."

Paulchen's gaze traveled round the room. "You've got so many books," he said and his eyes seemed to fill with anxiety. "I can't read," he declared and hunched his shoulders together as if he were freezing. "Books always make me nervous—anyway I don't see why they should go on printing them. No, no, no," he asserted zealously, making a gesture that was both timid and contemptuous at the books that lay open or with bookmarks on all the chairs, shelves and tables, "what's the point of them all? All they tell us is that people have it bad, but we know that already. A lot of them tell us the opposite, people have it wonderful—and we know that's so, in certain cases. There's getting to be less and less interest in books. Anyway, I couldn't care less about them—."

He had straightened up remarkably and even got to his feet. He walked to the mirror and arranged his artfully waved chestnut hair. Andreas observed that white face in the glass. How carefully the eyelashes were blackened, how exactly the narrow lips were outlined. But the thin inroads of sorrow had dug even more deeply around those lips in the meantime. Poor dancer's face—

Paulchen instantly fell silent before the mirror. Since Andreas said nothing, he had to speak, but his empty brain, never able to understand, found the same platitudes, the same expression as it had that night in the past: "Besides I don't get close to just anybody," he suddenly said and his lackluster eyes were unaware of the anxiety-filled light that was kindled in them. "Besides, there's lots of gentlemen and ladies running after me all the time. And the first time I saw you, I thought how cozy we'd be together and how much I liked you—but I still didn't think that."

Andreas wanted to make some reply, something consoling perhaps, but Paulchen was proceeding in a high, squeaky, startled voice. "I don't understand it at all," he babbled, not exactly sadly, but in perplexity, like someone who has lost his way. "Are you all that beautiful?—I'm still pretty too and I like what I see when I look in the mirror."—And since he could not understand why his blood was speaking so darkly and powerfully in him, he drew back against the wall, his eyes agog, like one pursued. "You'd never believe what I've been through these last few days," he shouted in his need, "I can't even enjoy myself any more. That Niels'll sleep with any woman. I know that Niels had put me in the shade. But I still feel so strongly about it. Do I disgust you?"

Andreas, who had just turned as pale as Paulchen, before his table, wanted to improve matters, explain, make everything all right. "But Paulchen," he said, and in confusion his hands began to arrange the books, "you mustn't talk like that—that's not right at all—I do like you—."

But Paulchen cut him off, stiff-necked, pained and uncomprehending. "That's not enough. I repeat, that's not enough!" And then he shouted into the room, his mouth wrenched open: "I love you—"

After that he could hide his face in his cool, beringed hands.

He could hear Andreas's voice beside him. "You're crying now," it comforted, "but everything will still be all right. You should be glad you're in love.-"—But Paulchen, not understanding, shook his head and sobbed. "You don't understand me," said Andreas and drew him over to a chair, "how could you dance if you didn't love?" But he stopped talking and fell silent all of a sudden. The sight of this body beside him, bent weeping and crumpled without knowing why, made any consolation seem flat and meaningless. Everything he had had to suffer on that night in the past and afterwards and was still suffering, he rediscovered in this poor, foolish sobbing and therefore gave up trying to remedy with words what was more deeply devastated than words could reach. Still, it might all have a happy ending.

It came rushing forth from between Paulchen's hands: "I don't dance any more—I can't dance ever again—." And the tears ran through his beautiful fingers and fell drop by drop onto his yellow shoes.—"You asked me before why I came here," he gushed wearily, "I came here to tell you this—nobody can blame me for that—"

When he took his hands from his face and stood up, his tears had dried. But something in his look had changed. "I still have to give you Fräulein Franziska's present," he said and handed him something small and flat, apparently a picture wrapped in tissue paper. "And this is for you too," he suddenly said quickly and unfastened a delicate gold bracelet.— Andreas merely said "Thanks"—with downcast eyes.—When he took Paulchen's cool, feather-light hand in his, their eyes met—Andreas felt as if for the first time. Paulchen's gaze had become harder, blacker and harder. But Andreas said nothing, Paulchen would not do anything foolish and suicide is always a crime against oneself. He only said "Goodbye," and the other one said "Goodbye," a brief, mysterious leave-taking between the two of them. It was as if one meant to say, "See you on the other side," and the other replied with his black gaze, "You'll be following me some day."—

Then Paulchen in his pleated lady's overcoat left with hurried little steps, his colorless face shadowed by the broad-brimmed fedora.

As Andreas was still standing erect at the table, he heard the sharp report of a revolver in the hallway. It was a snap rather than a detonation. And when the maids and women outside were running to the spot, he did not stir then either. With slow movements he took Fräulein Franziska's present out of the tissue paper wrapping.

Outside the cries of "My God! A doctor! Send for a doctor!" were growing louder. Without responding, Andreas heard every single sound. Now they were putting the body on a stretcher. But he stood there, holding a photograph of Niels, who looked out earnestly at him from a dark background.

5

Andreas dreamed in the presence of Niels's photograph.

It seemed as if he would find everything that had been dream, presentiment, passion and thought in himself repeated in the serenity of that face. It seemed as if the sorrow and chaste bliss of all creation had become flesh. And he did not know that to encounter all creation in one body is called "loving." He did not know that to love one voice means to hear and understand all melodies in one voice. After all, he had seen and felt the grass and trees as if for the first time, when he had first seen this man.

Andreas surrendered himself to this love, which he did not regard as an aberration. It never entered his mind to reject it or resist it as "decadence" or "morbidity." Such words have so little to do with the truth that they come from another world. Rather he well and truly pronounced this love good, he praised it along with everything that God had bestowed and ordained— however easy or heavy it was to bear.

For long hours his eyes were lost in that human face, more alien to him than any other and more intimate than any other. At last he seemed to recognize his own face in the other.

Mysteriously his own loneliness grieved out of the loneliness of those eyes. It was the same grief to be found in the sidelong glance of men without a country. It was the grief of the alienated.

One loved life in its resplendent, magnificent enigma, and all love for life was concentrated in love of the human body. But they would never wholly breathe as one with the beloved body, they too must remain aliens in the greater life in which their passion was to be consumed.

At this moment such was the wisdom of the youth who had sought death and withdrew from it at the command of a voice, in order to seek the innocence of life. Now he sat before a picture. But this alien, beloved visage melted away and was unfathomable in its silence.

Essentially, Andreas's heart had already realized that this was now an adventure—the most wonderful, richest in his young life—but that it was already almost over. He himself did not venture to explain this. He did not dare tell himself that he had to start his search all over again. It promised to be so hard—.

Then the smile that he had been endowed with as an antidcte to his need, that always came and always conquered when things were at their worst, appeared and said "it knew best" in the end.

This smile understood: we are never allowed to unite with the beloved body, the human body is alone for all eternity. But the love, which must renounce possession of the beloved, is perhaps great enough to aid the beloved body in its loneliness. This was the most that might be said.

This was his finest, his most private dream. The dream filled his heart with tenderness. The tenderness in him was like music.

So it was worth finding someone to give everything to without possessing him, to aid him and remain true unto death without possessing him. This was the wishful thinking of his intoxicated affection, this was the meaning of his misunderstood love and its great solution: aiding the loved one who is ever alien, training to remain close unto death. Then one could greet the ultimate, mysterious moment with joy. Then things would indeed become beautiful—in spite of it all.

The face was slipping away. Therefore it was worth recovering.

But, seeming to forget everything at once and to understand nothing essential, he suddenly placed his face against the cool glass of the photograph, as if this kiss were a surrogate for all that was more precious.

6

The dreaming, the silent isolation, the unhampered rambling of his thoughts disposed Andreas to gentleness. That was why he gave himself up to the wishes, passions, longings that at first he had so strictly rejected out of pride and defiance. He sat and dreamed about home. To dare to go home—

This time he would not spend his days at his father's villa beneath the scourge of unnatural tension and frustrated, repressed exertion. He had learned during these months. He had learned when, ravaged by vermin, he had wept in the room of the cab driver's wife. Learned, when he stood on a cabaret stage and was jeered at, and later welcomed Doctor Dorfbaum to his dressing room with the dexterity of someone wandering in a trance; learned infinitely much when, his face pressed against the rough linen, he had prayed at Niels's bedside.

He told himself that that had to be enough. He was the prodigal son who sits alone and forlorn among books in a hotel room and dreams of rest. Outside in the hall Paulchen had put an end to himself with a quiet click. It must be enough—

Towards evening his train would pull into the station in his home town. In the not very black but flat, shadowy darkness of nightfall, the arc lamps hang far apart from each other, yellow in his honor. A muffled sound, good-humored noises ring back at him. Of course they will be waiting for him on the platform. The spinster maid waves her hanky at him, acidulously cheerful at the sensation of his arrival. Marie Thérèse is there, charmingly dressed in a little gray riding hood. Naturally his father is not there to collect him—he is sedately waiting for him at home.—Marie Thérèse turns to him her bright little face with the rather overlarge mouth and tiny nose, crafty and yet innocent. Prattling as she comes, she extends the delicate and dirty little hands, which twitteringly confirm that she gave them a cursory wash earlier. Daintily she nestles close to him (not knowing that he is still "the prodigal son"), and he is so grateful to her for taking him by the hand and prattling as they slip out to the calèche—touching in its trustworthiness as it stands in the square before the station, conspicuously old-fashioned, and the old horses—a bay and a white—hold their heads so reverently bowed.—At home their father will be standing on the front steps, will wave and have forgot all his anger.

Andreas smiled and dreamed. "Then again, I might go for walks with Ursula towards evening on the outskirts of the city, where the fields are bare around the brickworks. We will stand on one isolated peak and look out over the city, lying before the evening sky with its many church steeples. The evening sky is cloudy and violet, but the dark is drawing in from the east. Ursula stands with her head bowed, her eyes shining in the red dusk."

Andreas stood up and walked over to the desk. "It is enough," he thought on his way, "I can rest now—"

He sat down and wrote, "Dear father—"

There was a knock at the door, the bellboy was bringing an express letter. It was addressed to Berlin and had been forwarded to him. The postmark read Paris.—Andreas's heart flew into his throat, although he did not recognize the handwriting. His hand trembled as he tore open the envelope. He forgot to sit down again, and read standing up in the middle of the room.

> "My dear Andreas! You may be surprised not to have heard from me for such a long time. I was traveling the whole time. I am now in Paris and live with Gert Hollström, she's a sculptor. My address is Rue Lepic—. Maybe you'll come for a visit.
> Regards Niels."

Andreas let the sheet of paper drop. He stared into space, as if listening to a great noise far away. His eyes were as fixed as the eyes of those who hear overpowering music and are wholly carried away by it.

He shuffled over to the telephone. He spoke slowly. "I would like to send a telegram—yes—to Paris, please. Herr Niels, Paris, Rue Lepic, care of Gert Hollström."—The desk clerk at the other end apparently asked something. Then Andreas smiled. "No, the gentleman's name is just Niels," he said with a smile, "that is his whole name.—The message is: Coming at once by plane. With you tonight."—The desk clerk repeated the name, the foreign address, the brief message. Andreas said "Thanks!" and hung up.

He laid his smiling face against the cool metal of the phone box. His body relaxed. Trembling all over, he laughed silently within.

He thought he had to do something now, get immersed in something. He rang for the bellboy who had brought the letter from Paris. The bellboy was a bit intimidated, for he thought he had put his foot in it or at least conveyed bad news, for which he would be harshly brought to book.

"What's your name?" the young gentleman asked sternly. "Fedor Meyer." "Your father's name?" "Viktor Meyer." "Your mother's name?" "Annaliese Meyer." "How old are you?" "Thirteen—."

Then Andreas laughed. "You are thirteen years old," he shouted, "you're a good boy—you are a good boy. Do you realize that you are a good boy? Maybe I'll come and pay you a visit. But then you don't live in Rue Lepic—."

He presented him with five stabilized marks and rather a great deal of milk chocolate. He complimented him on his mane of blond hair and circumstantially drew his attention to the fact that he had a famous namesake in Fedor von Zobeltitz.—The bellboy Meyer, who now realized that he was dealing with a harmless lunatic, cheerfully withdrew.

Later Andreas concluded the letter to his father, which was to have borne such a different message.

"Dear father!" the letter announced. "I had intended all last week to write you in more detail. You must not think that I have been silent out of ill will. I often think of you and Marie Thérèse and everybody. But life keeps one so busy, it makes such claims on one—"

He stopped in mid-sentence. He would not be walking with Ursula Bischof in the barren landscape. Ursula was his bride and she was waiting for him.

"But that is why it is often so beautiful," he went on writing.

7

A short time before he had to leave the hotel, after his suitcase was locked and he was sitting on a chair idly smoking a cigarette and ready for travel, a lady was announced and he instantly recognized the heavy, rather shuffling footsteps that approached his door.

Fräulein Franziska stood beside him in the dark red trilby and the iron gray tailored suit, as if they had never been apart for a moment. She was smiling just as she had when she so casually said "Pooh, pooh!" and "There, there" and took everything lightly.—Andreas was as terrified as if he were hallucinating. "So you're here too?" he asked and shook his head in bewilderment.—But she was already sitting down, without being offered a chair, and had taken off her hat; her mottled face had grown serious. "Yes, yes," she answered his question nonchalantly, while she scrutinized him through her squint, "I'm really glad that you're still here, downstairs the desk clerk told me you're planning to take a trip. The last few days in Berlin I couldn't get the notion out of my head that you'd be leaving Germany for a long time—." "Yes," said Andreas, "yes, I am definitely planning to. So you came only to say goodbye?"

She sat with her legs apart, her feet planted firmly before her. She looked at him gloomily from beneath her beetling brow. "No," her curt answer rang out, "I have something to tell you."

She rose and stood directly in front of him. Her stance was heavy and her clothes hung about her in remarkably messy folds. "Don't you notice anything?" she asked dispassionately, but rather more quietly, and looked down at the floor. "What do you mean? What do you mean?" he whispered, trembling in obscure anxiety on his chair.—Her face was the same as ever, her skin ravaged, her mouth brick red. Or had it become a stranger's face? A face he'd never seen before?—Then she said once more, very gently, almost imploring as she placed her hands in his: "Then you don't notice anything, Andreas?"—But all he said was: "I don't know—" and his hand trembled beneath hers.

Then she bent down to him and, as he closed his eyes in fear, she said in his ear, "I'm going to have a child, Andreas—"

Andreas was not alarmed, he merely squeezed her hand a little tighter. "Whose?" he asked quickly—and yet he knew whose name she would say. And she, very quietly in his ear: "Niels's."

Then they both had to smile.

"What was it like when you realized?" Andreas asked. "Did an angel come to you?"—But Franziska only replied, "I cried at first."

"When will it be born?" Andreas asked. "Six months from now." "And what will you call it?" "Andreas." "But what if it's a girl?" "It won't be—it doesn't dare be a girl."

And suddenly Andreas, opening his eyes and laughing out loud as if he had realized it for the first time: "Niels has begot a son!" "Our son!" said Fräulein Franziska and bent her mouth to the hands that lay on the chair arms. "Niels has begot our son—" Andreas whispered again, and his heart was filled to bursting with joy and great tenderness. "We shall bring him up, we shall raise him—watch him grow."—And suddenly by a peculiar association of ideas: "If only Paulchen could have lived to see it." And Fräulein Franziska opined: "He would have laughed. So very shrilly, the way he always did. 'I'm tellin' ya',' he would have screamed, 'we're doin' all right!'"

"He would have laughed," Andreas replied pensively. "Yes—yes—life—."

The golden chain he had been given as a "going away" present flashed dimly on his wrist.

* * *

They rode out to the airport together. They sat in the car leaning tightly on one another. Outside the suburban streets rushed by.

"Peterchen and Marie-Thérèse have probably lost their milk teeth by now, they've just got beautiful new teeth," Andreas said in meditation. And they stared ahead earnestly and self-importantly, caught up in the mystery of growth. Andreas suddenly recalled how he had first seen Niels in the skiff and how he had had to caress the trees, the grass and the great earth.

151

Fräulein Franziska put in her comment: "Little Andreas will get along nicely with Peterchen and Marie Thérèse. By the time he's seven, they'll be fourteen." "Yes," said Andreas, "my father had better be nice to him too—he is his grandson, after all."

Which made them both laugh.

They stood beside one another on the big airfield that lay gray-green and immeasurably wide in the wind. Nearby, rattling and whirring to an alarming degree, stood the plane that was to carry Andreas up and and into the storm in the cloudy sky.—A group of passengers walked up and down, with their hands behind their backs, cigars in their mouths, looking American in their gaudy woollen suits and brown leather coats. Suitcases were handed up. The propellers whirred.

"Do you think it's safe?" said Fräulein Franziska and smiled at him. "I am more worried about your coming to grief on a more important occasion," he replied with earnest chivalry.—Suddenly something else occurred to him. "I completely forgot to thank you for the picture you gave me— Niels's picture."—Then for the first time he saw that Fräulein Franziska could blush. "You're welcome—" she said quickly.

The group of passengers smiled indulgently at the honeymoon couple saying their goodbyes, although they looked rather funny, not to say a little suspect.—Andreas was still wearing the long camel's hair overcoat with the narrow waist and leather buttons that didn't match. Fundamentally he had not changed since, bowed beneath the burden of his suitcase, he had first taken the train to merciless Berlin.—And Fräulein Franziska always inspired general disquiet with her sinister eyes and brick red mouth.

When the plane's whirring had increased to a furious racket, they shook hands in parting. "All the best!" they both said, their faces turned to one another, as they walked backwards in opposite directions. "For whom?" they both asked at the same time.

Fräulein Franziska, who had suddenly begun to wave although Andreas was still on terra firma, said: "For Niels—" and Andreas had never mentioned to her that he was about to fly to him.

But, as all the bystanders laughed, Andreas shouted loudly across the field, "All the best for our child!"

FIVE

1

HE CAUGHT a taxi in front of his little Parisian hotel.
Rue Lepic, then—the car sped to bring him there. It
dashed so recklessly that Andreas had to shut his eyes.
Between half-closed lids he watched the city glide by, shimmering in its white splendor. The big city—. He opened his
eyes once, at the Place de la Concorde. And his eyes drank in
the shining expanse of the square as the car dashed across it.
But as soon as it turned into the Rue de Rivoli, where luxury
shops enticed beneath the arcades and Americans strutted in
checked suits, he half shut his eyes again.

But later the street grew steep and narrow. They were now
up in old Montmartre itself. Huffing and puffing, the car
labored upwards. It jolted, for the street was roughly paved.
Advertisements for cigarettes and cinemas appeared on the
wooden palings. But in front of the many little Mediterranean
bakeries and greengrocers' shops stood fat, dark haired
women, chambermaids and elderly landladies, parleying flu-
ently with each other across the street. This was Rue Lepic
itself, as he had imagined it: so steep, so filled with noises.

At the very top, at the end of the street, the taxi stopped. Andreas got out, paid—very slowly and mechanically as though in a dream—and stood before the house. It was gray, narrow and tall, with many little windows, most of them hung with colored curtains, pink and yellow in the gray of the sky; somewhat taller than all the adjacent houses, it towered in the pre-dusk glare of the sky.

The stairwell was black and rotting. Music, and not of the best, hit him in the face. An alto voice was practicing church music at an out-of-tune piano, and its sonorous up-and-down swells, its melting quavers came fluttering across to a new arrival like the exaggerated and over-emotional gladsome welcome of a nervous housewife.—But the higher he climbed, the more the melodies subsided into quietness.

Andreas climbed and climbed. The gray Montmartre house proved to be even higher than it had seemed from the outside. The silvery blue sky of early evening was already peeping through the dusty windows. The gray house was as high as a tower.

He rang where a sign read "Atelier." He waited a while, rang again, and heard steps coming towards him. In those last seconds it suddenly crossed his mind that the best thing to do would be to run away at the ultimate moment. He thought— and still stood motionless, waiting at the door.—"What am I doing here? He doesn't know me any more, doesn't remember me. He's even living with strangers—with a woman—." He was overcome with fear, ordinary, trembling fear, the kind one experiences during physical danger. Choking fear that ices the hands, clenches the stomach. Feverishly he computed how long it had been since he had seen him. "What's going to happen?" he thought and was rooted to the spot. "A little murder—a sensational item for the newspapers—."

Then the door opened. A tall individual stood across from him in the half-light. At first he thought it was a young man.

But she was already saying in a remarkably bright, clear voice: "You must be the friend Niels told me about?—Gert Hollström's the name"—and held out a large, but neatly modeled hand, on which a bright silver bracelet clinked.—The young man facing her in the vestibule spoke his name quietly: "Andreas Magnus—," and bowed his head a bit. And she responded with a free, friendly movement into the room: "Won't you come in?"

Andreas remained standing on the threshold to the atelier. All he saw was that the room he was supposed to walk into must be huge and painted pink. And somewhere there must be a big window standing open. The city's clamor could be heard rising upwards.—There were people in the room too, he heard voices. But he could not orient himself in this pink space or distinguish individuals.

His head teemed with very odd ideas, irrelevant ideas that sprang up in motley confusion. He made an effort to grasp and gather them, so that he could find a few phrases among them and say something—but then they submerged, sank back into black profundity, flew by like a flock of birds that suddenly plummeted, downed in meekness by a voice that reached him: very bright and yet a bit husky, shimmering with an inexpressibly acrid brilliance.—The voice reached him, as it had at that other time, as it always had, as it had since all eternity, close and yet evasive, intangible in the far distance. "Ah—here you are—," said the voice and laughed.

Niels turned his face to him. As Andreas had entered the room, he must have had his back turned away. He stood, legs apart, hands in his trouser pockets, opposite a sofa covered with ladies who were conversing with him. "Here you are—," he said and took a couple of steps towards him. They held one another's hands in the middle of the atelier.

The three ladies on the fantastically florid couch were also Scandinavians. With teacups on their laps, in little feathered hats as gaily colored as dickybirds on a perch, they chattered in ungrammatical and broken German, all at the same time— now and then suddenly twittering and openly burbling in their frivolous mother tongue. What a terrific darling they all thought him, this dear Niels, no, it was indescribable. "No!" they all shouted to each other in transports of delight—and their little voices broke and cracked sadly in this shrill exclamation.—"No! he's so funny!"—They clapped their hands, they turned their faces to each other, they laughed till they all had to cough into their snow-white handkerchiefs which hurriedly popped out of red, green and blue little pocketbooks.—Wasn't he half their compatriot, dear Niels? they conferred, laughing, with each other. Hadn't he told them his mother was Norwegian? Then too his pretty, his bright name. Yes, what hadn't he told them—! And eagerly bent towards each other, each hastily and awkwardly endeavoring to force her hanky back into her pocketbook, they were lost in the frivolity of their mother tongue.—Niels was back facing their stooped, snorting row, standing with his hair over his brow and his hands in his pockets.

In one corner, which was her work space, Gert Hollström sat among all her little creations in bronze, marble and white gypsum. The tarrying deer, leaping kangaroos, neighing colts surrounded her like ingenious children's toys. Among the animals stood a half-finished portrait bust of Niels.—While Niels and the foreign ladies were laughing, Andreas walked over to the sculptress and courteously chatted with her. "Excuse me for breaking in on you like this," he said somewhat stiffly, although correct in his black evening dress, "but since I was already in Paris, I naturally wanted to see Niels—" She only repeated, "Naturally—" and looked at him with blue-gray, steady eyes.—Suddenly she offered him honey bread from a china plate beside her. "You must be hungry," she opined objectively, "surely you can't have eaten anything before coming here—." And Andreas suddenly told her how he had come by plane—yes, through the air—

Gert Hollström was as tall and thin as a young athlete. She had the large-boned face of a somewhat Americanized but still charming young woman; she wore her hair very short at the nape of her neck and in bangs over her forehead almost down to her eyes. Her conversation with Andreas Magnus took a somewhat confusing turn. "I have really always regretted," she said and shook her head earnestly, "that our Niels hadn't joined the circus from the outset—naturally it's the only possible profession for him."—Was he now undergoing training, Andreas asked anxiously. And, a great sinewy youngster among her cavorting bronze animals, she replied, "Yes—didn't you know that? He has a workout on the trapeze with H.B. Monelli every day. But they're afraid he's already too old, and besides he lacks perseverance."—While they both smoked cigarettes, Gert Hollström spoke of the circus in general, the wrestlers, little Williams who had just had an accident—she did seem sorry as she related it, but her eyes gleamed brightly,—and eventually turned to her animals. "My horsie,"—she said and stroked the cool flanks of the prancing fillies as delicately as if they lived and breathed. In conclusion, she brooded—and bent her young face over the beasts—: "The body—yes, yes." And she and the young German smiled in the cigarette smoke pierced through by the sunlight.

The Scandinavians were leaving. They put aside their teacups and, looking rather small and plump as they stood up, they moved through the room in their spring outfits. They each wore a different color—one red, another blue, the third yellow. The outfits were all a bit summery for the middle of March, a bit flimsy. But they would come in handy in the summer. Embraces were exchanged, there was a grand leave-taking. Gert Hollström kissed each one's hand and had a civil little word for each. "Come again soon," she said—and the brightly colored little ladies laughed tipsily in reply,—"it was delightful as usual—." And then, escorted to the door by Niels, they were all outside. But hardly had their voluble twittering faded when Gert Hollström stretched out her strong arms. "Ah," she exhaled and tossed her head back, "women are nitwits—they're really ugly too—women are nitwits—," and laughed the curt, half-genuinely disgusted, half-mock contemptuous laugh of a man-of-the-world, sending her laughter up to the pink ceiling. Her hands were already in Niels's thick hair. "You're much better," she said—and clutched at it so firmly that she hurt him. "Ow, ow," he complained and twisted back his head as he went for her hair in revenge.—It was like puppies at play.

Then they all climbed the steep spiral staircase to the roof, for they wanted to see the big city from above. Hollström was the first in line, and as she took the steps with her long legs, her rust brown linen dress caught up, she went on lecturing on the worthlessness of a certain sex. "Anything connected with women is boring," she shouted angrily and pushed open the trap door to the roof balcony.—They stood at the top, their eyes dazzled.

Fuzzily, dissolved in immensity, the city lay bright and broad at their feet like a body of water. Its noises, violently blurred, rose out of the peculiar white mist that lay over it. Certain noises sporadically stood out from the chaotic, mysterious whole. An auto horn called up to them like an abrupt, almost terrifying question.—Might it have been a human voice?—It had been seized by some wind and its sound was borne out of the noisemaking chorus they were over-hearing.

Gert Hollström stared straight ahead with bright eyes and did not seem aware that the lives of millions were summed up in the darkness at her feet. A harder, merrier frivolity—a proud frivolity—a new frivolity shone in her eyes.—Her hands, capable of shaping lusty animal bodies, were clutching the gaudy silk scarf she had thrown around her neck and that framed her face. Above these grasping hands her mouth was tightly pursed.—Niels stood earnestly, very earnestly, touchingly pressed to her side, and his gaze, which looked over the city which was not his homeland, held no question, no searching either, certainly no questing, just a slight melancholy, a remote, evasive sadness darkened his clear serenity. What was this grief, whence came this inexplicable sorrow?—Not from thinking, certainly not from thinking. Then it must derive from somewhere deeper inside.

Andreas, standing beside him with his eyes downcast, asked quietly, "Do you like living in this city? Are you at home here?"—And wanted his question to imply something quite different, which he could not express otherwise.—But Niels turned his face to him as if he failed to understand the plain meaning of the words. He looked straight at him, almost in reproach, as if the questioner were trying to make fun of him.—Then Andreas's gaze slipped from this face which could provide it no haven or resting place, but remained unintelligible, straightforward, simple, mysterious in its grief.—

Gert Hollström suddenly began to compute how long she had lived in this city—Paris. Two and a half years it was now. But she wanted to go to America soon.

Andreas said he had to go now and, high up on the roof, they made a date for that evening. There was to be an artists' party where they would meet again. Nine o'clock, then, at the front entrance. Andreas was already climbing into the shaft of the spiral stairs, so that he was visible from the chest up. "See you this evening," Gert Hollström called again and waved her big hand; released, the kerchief fluttered in the wind. But Niels was already looking out over the city again and paid no attention as Andreas disappeared through the trap door.

For one last moment Andreas saw him standing tall, his

hands clasped to his chest. He stood as he had always known him: in blue trousers and an open shirt. His mouth was half-open, as if it were drinking in the fresh air like wine.

Then Andreas accepted the darkness of the stairs.

2

He went in all directions through another couple of streets which kept getting narrower and narrower. But he paid no attention to his steep path until it stopped short. Now he was at the summit of the city apparently, and there was nowhere farther to go. It was a steeply inclined field, half covered with trash and stones. Old people and fat nursemaids with trouble-some babies were sitting in the field. They had been warming themselves while the sun still shone and now they sat on the sparse greenery amid the rubble, looking at the city, too languid to get up even though the sun had gone down some time before.

Behind the steep flat field was a church, big and broadly arched with white domes. At first it seemed of recent construction, built here not long before—round and broad like a mosque.—Andreas stood by it, terror in his heart. A white church above the city—.

The little stall must be here somewhere, smelling of incense and filled with the appliances of devotion.—He felt almost no surprise when he found it. He calmly met the watery blue gaze of the young saleswoman, oddly and sentimentally cast from below. Evidently she was deaf and dumb, but they had no difficulty coming to an understanding. The black rosaries hung in such thick rows next to each other. They were certainly more expensive than might have been expected. The young lady carefully put away the money she took in a black purse. "Pour les pauvres enfants"—she murmured with a tied tongue. At least Andreas now knew that his munificently offered money was intended for benevolent purposes.

It had rapidly grown dark by the time he left the stall. A cool March evening. But these roads seemed lit from within. Silvery white, they ran from the church down to the city, which was starting to light up below with its first artificial illumination.

The rosary twined round his hand, Andreas crossed the city, whose noise rose up in the pale quiet of the darkness and was like an admonition, indeed, a challenge.

These spring evenings were still cool. The moon was frozen too, a crescent curved in upon itself in terror.

Andreas had to hurry to get home to his little hotel. He had to change for the international artists' party.—Tightly wrapped in his overcoat he moved rapidly downhill on the shimmering path that led from the church to the city.

***

As he was let out in front of the dance hall, a second car, driven by a tall lady, stopped at the door at the same time. A very elegant young man in a top hat and white opera cape got out of the coupé behind her. Beneath the red lamplight that lured like a huckster in a market, the three greeted each other: Gert Hollström, Niels and Andreas Magnus.

While Hollström turned in her heavy mantle at the cloakroom and suddenly reappeared as a long legged, colorfully befeathered Indian chief, Niels, his walking stick pert beneath his arm, greeted acquaintances who rushed prattling by, in fur capes with Pierrot ruffs comically sticking out of them. Above the narrow collar of his dress suit, his blond face was like that of a jolly baroque angel.

As a threesome they strode down the corridor that led to the reception rooms: Gert in the middle, Niels on her left, and Andreas on her right arm.

The corridor was lined with little ashtrays filled with aromatic burning incense. The walls were painted in bright colors like the backstage areas in operetta theatres. The trio walked slowly down the red trail to the ballroom.

They were greeted by perfume, human noise and jazz music.

3

This was "Clo-Clo-Clo," the artists' festival—the most fashionable assemblage of wild, international bohemian types—the brilliant ball for intellectual society that also liked to have a good time—.

This was the place for fun, enough fun to make you die laughing. This was where Europe, the "pick" of the whole world, threw itself a dazzling, hilarious scream of a party.

Arm in arm, the trio walked through the rooms, in the middle the garish Indian, whose reddish-yellow feathers waved proudly over her head, the lads in evening dress to the right and left. They strolled among the dancers to the tables, where people sat bawling beside champagne buckets, and shoved their way past.

The expanses of wall were covered with gaudy posters, clippings from comic papers, all sort of extravagant caricatures and captions, fastened with thumb tacks. A signpost of extraordinary size pointed to the toilets, with a crudely sketched ballerina smirking lewdly at those in search of them; cyclists were pedaling away on enormous sports posters; and the busts of famous boxers with broad cheekbones were highlighted in front of a black velvet drape. A different band was blaring in each room, the crazily orchestrated tunes mingled with each other to the point of perfect cacophony. While one sighed a lugubrious tango, another boomed a demoniacally negroid march. In the next room, however, a tiny, dolled-up female dwarf, encircled by a throng of laughing spectators, was singing her particular hit tune. As if her diminutive size was not enough, she stuttered, and everyone joined in the chorus of her song, rudely mocking her speech defect—which seemed to make her all the happier. "Sur les côteaux—" they burbled, and the merry monstrosity hopped in their midst.—But a Russian tart was screaming her own number from a side box, apparently already dead drunk and probably thinking that the dwarf below was singing the same song. She flung her arms about and screamed beneath her red plumed hat while her big bosom wobbled: "Je cherche après Titine, Titine ma cousine—."

Every language in the world tangled with every other and French was hardly predominant. Young Spaniards in garish outfits gesticulated crudely, rolled their R's frightfully and arched their gloomy eyebrows. The Russian ladies, fat and voluptuously made-up, danced a lot with each other, although they were so stout they could barely catch hold of their partners; they behaved with dissolute silliness in the wild press for pleasure, which their sluggish natures so seldom understood.—The gaiety of the little Scandinavian women cooed aloft, as they swore to their partners in faltering French that they were already quite drunk—drunk through and through.— While the Japanese painters were bleating oddly and getting seriously enraged with one another, tall blacks, squeezed pathetically into evening dress, were holding slender Parisian cocottes in their colossal arms.—The extremely grizzled gentleman in the tuxedo over there was an American millionaire; four or five Russian or French women had just lain down at his feet.—There were the two old Englishwomen, who held lorgnettes to their eyes and strutted through the crowd in odd silk outfits, enjoying the view, although people joked viciously behind their backs. "Les Amairicaines, les Amairicaines"— people tittered and told jokes about them.—But how the group from Vienna was enjoying itself! They were all wound round with paper streamers and doubled up with delight. "No!" they would shout time and again, "how brilliant—how brilliant—" and choke with laughter.

The German men of letters sat in their corner and among themselves insulted their imperiled homeland, which no one wished more evil to than they. "Somebody tell me, what good is that country?," shouted one, the skinny, swarthy one with the horn-rimmed spectacles, "what good is it, what does it want?—A tasteless troublemaker, that's all—." And when the fat, well-meaning one suggested, "What about Hölderlin— you're forgetting Hölderlin and Stifter," the radical only waved maliciously and held up his hand in exasperation. "Literature—literature—" he said sourly and the others nodded in agreement behind their champagne glasses.

Meanwhile the model from Poland had leaped on a table covered with a white cloth. She swung an absurdly small liqueur glass through the air and, without the slightest pretext, shouted the "Marseillaise" into the hall. "Allons, enfants—." Only the German men of letters sang along in cracked, tone deaf voices, the ones in the horn-rimmed glasses nodding like owls.

A Jewish picture dealer from Berlin hailed Gert, Niels and Andreas. "The three Graces!" he said with a Jewish accent, sweating in his red Pierrot costume. But Hollström, who had stopped bothering to speak German, replied with something incomprehensible in Norwegian. He seemed from the outset to be most concentrated on Niels, whose backside he tried to pinch.

They were soon lost in the crush. The atmosphere between Niels and Hollström had in any case become a bit strained, without Andreas aware of any reason for it. Now the group of little Norwegian ladies danced around the sculptress and tossed confetti and bright-colored cloth flowers at her. For once she had to behave like a gentleman to them, and, erect in their motley midst, she swung her tomahawk in a warlike manner.—A dress designer from Vienna laid hold of Andreas, who let himself be dragged into a dance as if he had no will of his own. "You caught my eye right from the start," she said and pressed her overpoweringly perfumed body sentimentally against his. It turned out that she was there on assignment from a fashion journal and now and again would zealously draw rapid costume sketches in a red silk notebook. "All Europe is throwing a party," she said and pulled the dancer closer to her. As they danced, she had deliberately jostled a hot-tempered Spaniard and he was now theatrically insulting them behind their backs.

Even a carousel had been set up in one large room. Silvery and tinkling, with lots of little white horses, it circled round and round. All the shrieking ladies, clasping their arms round the horses' necks, displayed their well-turned silken legs. The grizzled American was to be seen galloping on one of the silver steeds to general laughter—he looked like a comic baron in a fairy tale.—In the quieter corners of the room, decently dressed youths moved about offering indecent photographs in open wrappers to any gentleman who seemed well-to-do. "Très cochon," they whispered as a recommendation, "indeed," they said quietly—for their prospects were all foreigners, Englishmen or Americans, "très cochon—." Single ladies sat here too, intently bent over their compact mirrors with lipstick, eye shadow and powder puffs.

An uproar suddenly broke out in one of the main rooms. A child's face emerged above the waves of the crowd—someone was being uplifted in triumph. A shout grew clearer and clearer, as it carved a path for itself and took on form.—The energetic picture dealer form Berlin had pushed Niels into a chair, joined forces with a drunken painter, and now the two were dragging along the utterly stupefied youth. "L'enfant du siècle," they shouted at him and turned blue in the face. "Messieurs, messieurs—voilà l'enfant du siècle!" Although no one understood exactly what they meant, no one appreciated the nonsensical homage of the two fat gentlemen to this youth—they all shouted along, infected and electrified: "L'enfant du siècle—voilà" rang through the rooms. "Vive l'enfant! Vive notre enfant du siècle."—And Niels, now upheld by many arms, laughed like a drunkard, with no idea of the meaning of it all. His bow tie had come undone and his shirt front had popped out. But the dazzling light of the chandelier played a glittering game in his disheveled hair.—The stuttering she-dwarf danced around him, still rejoicing, like a jester possessed before the Ark of the Covenant. The Russian women, their make-up running down their faces, bent forward and clapped their hands, so that the patent fasteners on their silk dresses snapped apart, letting them fall wide open. The shouts of the Spaniards became an enthusiastic howl of rage. The Japanese with shrewd mouse faces squealed shrilly at it, the Viennese enjoyed it wrapped in paper streamers and blissful amid the clamor, but above all the voices of our Norse ladies hung like the confused twittering of birds, the most joyous and brainless song of the lark. Only the American galloped stalwartly on his tinkling steed, surprised that no one was paying him any more attention. Only one of the unescorted ladies turned away, making use of this desertion to come up to him with business-like entreaty: "Écoutez, monsieur," she said quickly, and then she wanted a hundred francs on the spot.

The cyclist pedaled away on the wall. The lady smirked obscenely over the toilets. In all the rooms all the jazz bands blared a fanfare, and all the painters, men of letters, fashion designers and actors, all the tarts and craftswomen jubilated in the language that was least their mother tongue, burbled to the ceiling an almost imbecilic homage to someone they did not know. "Vive l'enfant du siècle!"—Then too, Andreas was dancing, holding his loquacious Viennese in his arms. She tactlessly rattled on about it, saying she felt as if she were experiencing an historic moment first hand, although it was only a carnival stunt, an international bohemian joke, and she did not notice that the man in her arms who "caught her eye right from the start" now had to contend with tears.

One of the tall Englishwomen, however, stood on tiptoe behind Niels and pressed into his hair a large garland which she had speedily bought at a nearby florist's. "Oh wonderful, wonderful!" her lanky lady friend whispered at that and shook her head emotionally.

Then Niels sprang off his triumphal chair. Confused by the laughter and giddiness, he leaned over to one of the fat gentlemen, while all the ladies pressed around, exuding perfume. "Ah, quelle beauté! Quelle belle jeunesse!" they whispered around him, and the picture dealer, who had occasioned it all with his noise, tousled Niels's hair.

But Niels, pulling loose from him, finally came up with a word and a retort. Laughing, he brushed the hair out of his eyes and, as he sought to escape through the crush, he shouted in the most ringing voice to them all: "You're crazy!!"—and was gone.

* * *

This was "Clo-Clo-Clo," the artists' festival—the most fashionable assemblage of wild, international bohemian types— the brilliant ball for intellectual society that still liked to have a good time. Anyone would be upset not to be there. It had been advertised with absurd publicity, but in its luxurious abandon- ment it actually surpassed all expectations. All the celebrities were on hand. People pointed out the tall, hatchet-faced painter who was tippling in a corner. A much-talked-about poet was dancing with a kinky-haired negress. The American ran the carousel and the Viennese were in seventh heaven. A she-dwarf had been procured, chansons had been sung, and the rich Englishwomen had adorned "l'enfant du siècle" with roses.

What more could there be? What was yet to come?—
Sensation upon sensation—. The boxer, whose portrait bust
with broad cheekbones stood before a white cloth, genially
appeared in person, shook the hands of all the celebrities and
was joyously welcomed. Somewhere a famous soprano was
performing romantic art songs as best she could, while a
couple of step-dancers were carrying on with little bowler hats
and grotesque noses in the next room. The atmosphere
became even more thickly condensed, couples were already
tightly entwined on the staircase.—Amid the commotion the
Viennese dress designer fanned a breeze at her partner with
black ostrich plumes. The she-dwarf made a progress through
all the rooms—a flirtatious, hunched demon in her dress of
golden mail.

Then a second uproar broke out, a second disturbance
occurred. Once again the eye of the storm was the fair-haired
fellow with the ringing voice, who had earlier been celebrated
without knowing why. Obviously he had to be the center of
attention.—

It had begun with a verbal exchange. Two persons were
having a rather violent discussion, the fair-haired youth and
the lanky squaw, but there was nothing especially unusual
about that. "I'm not going there again!" cried the youth. "I'm
not going on with that disgusting training any more! All day
today my body felt wrecked! I care too much about my body
for that!" he shouted and laughed angrily. But the long-legged
lady retorted, "Why do you care so much about your body?!—
You're flabby, that's all there is to it. I'm telling you this, right
here, in front of all these people: if you stop working in the
circus, I'll throw you out of my house!"—To which he replied,
"Oho!" and tossed his head back.—Unchecked they flung
insults at one another. The bystanders began to laugh, a group
began to collect. "Why do you care so much about your
body?!" the woman screamed again, and the feathers waved

over her flushed face.—"Do you really know why you were raised on high just now?—You're the boy whore of all Paris!!" she howled at him as if in triumph. And her eyes, which had become glowing flints in her raging frivolity and quivering lust for battle, met his brighter, flashing eyes. Around them, the little Frenchwomen were poking fun: "Ah—les allemands—ils disputent—," and pointed their fingers at them.

But before anyone was aware, the two of them were rolling on the carpet, entangled in a ball. How they pummeled one another! Now one was on top, now the other. Now the woman lay full-length on top of him and had seized him by the hair and was banging his head against the floor. "Why do you care so much about your body?" she shouted into his face. And, bestial with pain and rage, he bellowed inarticulately at her.— Uneasiness began to creep into the pleasure with which people had been watching this amusing fist fight and boxing match. Loud were the cries for waiters to come and part the now bleeding contenders. "Garçon! vite, vite, garçon!!" the poor cocottes wailed and hid their faces in their hands, for they could not stand the sight of blood. Others, however, wanted still more, and clapped and stomped, while the journalists, with their nose for disaster, had pulled out their notepads. And now the youth was kneeling on her as she lay on the ground, and his knees pressed down her shoulders. She'd be lucky if he didn't punch her in the face with his fist. But now it was his turn to deal out insults—for he was on top and had right on his side. "You seduced me!" he howled, sitting on her—and blood poured down his brow.—"Why did you pick me up?! Why did you wear me out?!—She said she loved me!" he jeered in rage above her. "What does that matter to us?—Why do I care so much about my body?—It's too good for you!!!"—And then, suddenly, as he struck at her again with both fists: "Female! Female!!"—But the fact that she lay beneath him so silently stretched out so long and still, sobered him. He arose, stood perplexed at her side, and his patent leather shoes were flecked with blood.

Then someone behind him took him gently by the shoulders. A voice said quietly, "Come on!"—and as a pathway nervously opened for them through the masked throng, someone led him away and to the exit.

Andreas and Niels walked down the red passage together, with no one trying to stop them. Andreas had put an arm around the shoulders of the bleeding man, who, in an overcoat hastily draped over him in passing, involuntarily leaned on him like one dead tired. Andreas began to feel nervous facing this strange look whose blue had almost darkened to black beneath the bleeding brow; it seemed to gaze vaguely beyond things, unfathomably above them.

Meanwhile in the ballroom an ever more timid circle formed around Gert Hollström, who, like a wretched school-boy who has been soundly thrashed, streaming blood, cowered on the ground and sobbed into her big hands.

4

Then they sat beside one another in the dark rattling car. "Now you can't go back to her either—," said Andreas and dared not look at him. But he was already laughing again—though in a peculiar way Andreas had never heard before. "No," was all he said, "that's all over now."—

Andreas asked him again, "Now what? Do you have any idea what you'll do now?"—But he got no reply.

Niels had shaken a little paper cone of white cocaine onto the back of his hand. He carefully carried the back of his hand to his nose. He sniffed.

After that Andreas hardly dared to talk to him any more. Because his eyes were so darkened from within. Because he sat by his side so unfathomably silent and alien. Andreas had to think of little Boris, waiting gentle and numb at the Garden of

Eden for someone to pick him up.

But suddenly Andreas did speak. "You're going to have a child," he said abruptly, and gently touched his hand, "listen—Franziska is going to have a child by you soon—we shall have a son—."

But Niels just sat there, somewhat sunk into himself and lightly jolted by the ride. The blood on his forehead had congealed by now, but the hair hung disheveled over it. The mouth which was half-open as if drinking in the darkness was wreathed by a smile: imperishable, impermanent, impenetrable. His opera cape hung in great folds about him like a crusader's mantle. The necktie dangled disreputably, the square cut shoes were hideously soiled.

But what was this smile conveying, what did it know? Was it smiling at the child it had begot and hoped would survive? Or was it only the stupor of the narcotic that lay around these lines?

Andreas wanted to believe that its blissful remoteness testified to the mystery of the body which is alone—the sweet mystery of the body.

5

Stop here, Niels suddenly called to the driver, they wanted to get out here and walk around a little—here at Les Halles.—

The cabman, accustomed to all sorts of foolishness, did not quibble over that, but took his money and drove away. "Yes—Les Halles—they're the most beautiful thing in all Paris—" Niels said rapidly, though with an oddly heavy tongue. "They are the most beautiful thing—in all Paris!" he repeated and laughed curtly.

He stood in the black opera cape in the middle of the street. He had definitely lost his hat somewhere. He was not drunk, but there was something uninhibited about his movements, and his eyes, staring at the ground, could not be seen. Andreas thought of a great many others—of evil white powder and blood running down brows,—but after a slight pause he suddenly said, only to have something, anything to say: "Les Halles—they're still 'the belly of Paris'—." But Niels failed to understand this. "Then let's go," was all he said abruptly, and they walked down the street beside one another.

It was a narrow street they headed down, jammed with piles of vegetables. Not very far away the street debouches into a square, whose brightness can already be glimpsed in the distance.

Niels is loud and talkative. He buys a bunch of radishes from a wrinkled iron-gray little woman who sits waxen over her vegetables to prevent them from being stolen.—He haggles with the Spanish fruit vendor for his oranges, which the man stubbornly refuses to sell, sticking obstinately to the assertion that it is forbidden at night. Niels, in uncertain French, brings in the iron-gray little old woman, who had been ready and willing to deal in her radishes—but the Southerner, his head tilted skeptically, raises the palm of his hand in a Jewish gesture of doubt, as if to point out what a shocking amount of deceit there is in the world.—Niels has to prolong the unfinished business. But now he wants to have a brandy at that little dive, he walks in and the unkempt women behind the bar all laugh, for his tie dangles so loosely. Leaning across the bar towards them, he simply laughs along and even asks, as he puts the darkish brandy glass to his lips, "Nous sommes drôles, n'est-ce pas?"—and forces Andreas to drink. But the polite barmaids all giggle as they raise their hands in protest: "Oh, pourquoi—pourquoi, messieurs? Pourquoi drôles? Mais non, messieurs—," at which they shake all over with laughter, and the lads tippling in the background laugh along as does the fat red barkeeper.

But then they both step into the square, which lies with unnatural brightness in the light of the arc lamps. They both stand still for a moment, as if they doubted the reality of what was before them. It was like an enchanted little market town, where, in the fashion of the night, hands move in the lurid light amid the bright-colored fruits and vegetables. What a fairy tale trade!

Women are sitting here too, rotund and humorous in their Mother Hubbards, guarding the little piles of appetizingly symmetrical potatoes. Little gray men trundle wheelbarrows of cabbages back and forth. Everywhere comestibles are being unloaded, stacked and sorted.

It might be four o'clock or four-thirty by now. A blueness is already waking in the night sky. It shines out of the great blackness with a deep purple and spreads. In this blazing purity before sunrise, the sky is as chaste as at the glassy hour after sunset, when day and night touch in lingering affection.—

Here are the big, black, vaulted entrances leading into Les Halles proper, where sales will take place by day. Here is the meat market.—Niels and Andreas walk arm-in-arm without a word past the bloody calves which hang side by side in long rows with their gaping bellies slit open. This is what the city feeds upon.—New ones are being collected on high racks: plenty of meat, bleeding flesh. The air reeks densely.—Niels sniffs it in like a beast, he smiles formally at it. "Meat," he says and breathes deeply, "yes—that's what flesh smells like—" Strong fellows hammer and pound great axes on the bloody carcasses of animals. Their eyes are defiant as they work, their blood-spattered sleeves have been rolled up, the muscles bulge on their arms. Little splinters of bone fly about.—Here hang pigs, fat, with defeated human eyes. Here hares with drooping ears. This is the way flesh smells. And now they have reached the live fish.

Suddenly Niels and Andreas are in the flower market. There the electric lights play shimmeringly over all the plants.

The flower vendors sit behind their bright-colored heaps and entice the young gentlemen to buy. "Écoutez, messieurs! Des fleurs fraîches!"—And Andreas suddenly buys. He buys flowers for Niels, who has not asked for them, white lilacs and slender yellow roses and flaming carnations. Niels already has his arms full of them, but Andreas has to have still more. "They're beautiful—oh, what a smell the violets have!" he cries, suddenly animated, and Niels, who only laughs, has to carry the many small bunches of violets as well. "It's too much—leave off!" he warns. And he lays his blood-stained face against the fresh flowers. They are sprinkled with water— or is it dew? He feels his cheeks are wet and has to laugh at that.

The flower women have their fun with their young customers. "Ah—les deux flâneurs!" they shout lustily, "voilà les deux flâneurs!" and laugh into their wrinkles, while they brandish the red, yellow and blue blossoms in commendation. But one especially shrewd and teasing woman cries out the roguish question: "Ou *un* flâneur avec son bel ami?"—and doubles up laughing.—And even the gendarme who stands in stately magnificence among the hampers puts a hand to his cap and affably declares, "Ah—on s'amuse à notre Paris—."

Yes, they are two charming loiterers, out for a stroll after a night of harmless merriment, laden with flowers among the working classes. They are greeted with good will, for they look so amusing. They are both laughing.

Now they walk among the vegetables. It smells almost as strong here as in the meat market. The asparagus lies in savory bunches, and the heads of cabbage, green and blue, are stacked in high pyramids, and there are piles of spinach and yellow rape, and then comes the fruit. What an aroma the apples give off! They must have just been picked from the tree.

The two walk much more slowly, the place becomes unpopulated. Where are the wrinkled ladies, where are the strong fellows and the little gray men? The fruit lies under the electric lights, deeply silent and aromatic.

As Andreas, his head bowed, was lounging behind, he suddenly noticed that Niels was no longer walking at his side.—As soon as his eyes anxiously sought him out, they found him, already at a distance, walking slowly back and forth among the silent piles of vegetables. He was retreating into the stillness of the potent earthy smells, his arms full of flowers against which he laid his bloodied face, his gaze darkening.

But Andreas did not have the right to follow him.

Then he felt that a woman was standing beside him. He turned around and looked into her painted face. Alien, stark and impartial, it confronted him with its black, upstanding hair and brick red lips. He did not know the woman, it was not Fräulein Franziska. But she knew all about him.—She was wearing down-at-heel boots and a grotesque feathered hat. Below this feathered hat her voice came to him coarsely, coarse and full of kindness. She only said—and pointed her hand at the man walking back and forth without stopping amid the fruit. "Il ne revient pas." And shook her head.

Then Andreas turned quickly towards the disappearing figure. Won't he show him his face just once more? He raised both hands in a timorous gesture of anguish, as if it might still be possible to stop him.—But he was no longer to be seen. The darkness, redolent of fruit, had already taken him away.

When he tried to say something to the woman, she too was gone. He saw her in the distance: her backside, estimable, broad and eloquent, was wobbling away. She strode slowly out of the yellow flicker of the arc lamps they were standing under, and into the dawn.

No one could be spied, as far as the eye could see. Andreas wondered how he would find his way again out of all the cabbage and spinach.

*

How white and pale the little hotel room lay in the morning light! The beds in this country were broad, in the prospect of strenuous lechery.

He sat down on the wide bed. He wondered whether he should undress and lie down to sleep or ring for breakfast and begin the day briskly. The wide bed drew him to it.—But next to the bed, on the night table, stood the photograph of Niels that poor Paulchen had once had to bring with him to Cologne.

Then weary Andreas realized what he had to do. He stood up and went across the room to the table. There on the checked tablecloth lay the rosary. It had been looped back upon itself like a holy grass snake, coiled and silently waiting. But he lay hold of it, it twined itself around his hand. He walked back across the room with it to the bed. And slowly, full of solicitude, like someone performing a sacred rite, he placed the black chain round Niels's earnestly gazing picture. It was now adorned.

Then he sank back on the bed, in evening dress as he was.—And he closed his eyes.

At first he heard the beating of angels' wings. He could not open his eyes and so he could not see the angels. But he felt their closeness, the silvery sound of wings and musical instruments, their holy speech without sounds. They crowded round him, the whole room was now filled with them. They must be walking through the walls, the whole hotel room was filled with angels, the throng thickly clustered around the weary man in his wide bed.

Then, out of their midst, strode She, whose unapproachable grace had once rejected his offering. At that time her words had been as curling smoke in the night air. "Thou hast not yet deserved it. Thou hast not yet suffered. Thou hast never yet understood me—"

But now she came over to him. Now she stood at his side,

rich in grace amid her garment's folds of drapery. He had not brought the offering to her, he had lain the ornament which she had once rejected around another's beloved picture today.—If one simply loves: is that not sufficient token of esteem for her?

Now she bent down to his brow. Now her face was above his. Then he thought he recognized it: was it not as kindly as a mother's, gentle as a lover's after the first night, mysterious as the face of a sister?

While the soundless speech of angels rose around him to become the song of a heavenly choir, the dreamer fell unconscious.

***

But as the bright light of morning streamed into his room, he was already sitting at his desk over a letter. Before his departure he was writing to Ursula Bischof. The letter read:

"When I come back, my dear Ursula, I shall tell you everything—and I shall indeed come back. Certainly in the near future I still have much traveling in prospect and much wandering abroad. I am traveling south from here and then across the sea. I have a desire to see the whole world, the whole gaudy globe. I will travel to the far East, where everything originated, and to America, where industry is breaking it all up again. I should like to observe everything, everywhere, all types of humanity. When I then come home—perhaps then I can paint beautiful pictures that breathe wind and desire and sorrow. But I do not believe that the future has anything to do with pictures. Neither pictures nor books. I cannot see into the future, the future has nothing to do with me. But if I let myself stray once more in that direction, I have a dark vision of what art and its right to life will encounter in the next few years. I have a dark vision too of what the great, most intimate dream our best men dream of, the dream of a morally free, deeply conscious and happy humanity, will encounter. The unrest of our times is great and powerful, yes, perhaps no other times ever knew so great an unrest and a stirring in all directions as our own. Where all this, this great dance, will lead is known to us least of all.—I fear that a spiritually inspired human society and an ideal republic are the least likely results. We can have no information on how to solve this unrest; perhaps the solution will simply come from the great abyss, the apocalypse, a new war, a suicide of mankind. But the greater and more powerful the unrest, the holier will be the subsequent silence. Commotion is on the verge of becoming peace. Life is on the verge of becoming death. Are we such aimless dancers that we celebrate life as a pious festival and fail to consider how we may turn it to the good, the true, the able? Then we should be forgiven, it is not easy these days to serve any kind of order. Besides a festival is not something frivolous or chic or thoughtless. The vestigial meaning of such a festival can always be kept in our hearts. So it seems to me no transient merrymaking or child's play, but an earnest game, a pious adventure.

"Dear Ursula, my dear bride—I am writing these words to you, but perhaps you know more about them yourself. I only felt that I had to share them with you. You will not hear from me again for some time. All the trees are rustling for me, all the seas are waiting for me. There are people sitting in their parlors whom I must meet in the near future. The human body is beautiful in all places. I love the human body—."

He glanced over at the picture that stood before him, the picture of Ursula and her father. As he wrote, his father looked at him with warm, yet knowing eyes. And Ursula's feminine gaze met his, caressed him, gave him a sense of well-being.

He tossed the pen aside and leaped up. He would finish writing it down South.

Now he had to pack, to be off again on his travels.

He went into the street and the car with his suitcases packed in it was already waiting. The porter in his green apron was rubbing his hands—had his tip been big enough to cause hand-rubbing?—The garrulous concierge waved from her lodge and called, "Au revoir, monsieur, au revoir—," full of merriment, though her face was very faded. The blonde chambermaid suddenly turned out to be from Alsace and spoke fluent German. "The German gentlemen are all so friendly," she said and nodded dreamily.

The driver extended a clever face with a black, drooping mustache and wittily expressive almond eyes. Had the lady in the lodge stopped waving at him with her white lace handkerchief?

Andreas got in, sat somewhat cramped among the four suitcases and the single overnight bag—why deny it?—even poked a little bruise into his shinbone. But how quickly the car traveled, although loaded so heavily. A trim car, a bright gray, neatly designed car. A clever driver with a drooping mustache, Chinese variety. Probably an erstwhile speculator in stocks and bonds, naturally went bankrupt, witty, indeed roguish despite misfortune, not turned grouchy and discontented. How he was whistling now—.

Then the streets glided by. A whole train of soldiers came towards them. Students in grass-green caps came towards them, speaking English—one could hear them. A boy was playing ball, all by himself. A boy in blue shorts with long, thin legs and a fringe of hair like a village idiot's almost hanging in his eyes.—In all his brief boy's life had he ever been so urgently loved as at this drunken moment when Andreas rode past him?

Andreas had taken off his hat. The wind had gripped his hair and blew through it. Andreas's face took on the look of a runner, rushing across the fields towards a great forest. Wind in his hair and a confused smile on his lips.

That was the sky of day, he had seen it turn blue above the fruit and vegetables. This was air, the wind's air blowing into his face.—Which way should he run? Where would it end? What would it be like at the finish—and what would come of it?

Then, in the jolting car, he suddenly clasped his hands, penned in among his suitcases. But his piety was distilled into a fresh formula, a mysterious thought, which was: I believe in this world. He did not quite understand what he meant by that and how he had managed to arrive at it. But it had not been easy.

With wind-blown hair and clasped hands his eyes rested on the men going by, and they looked back at him laughing and he was a runner, praying.